Biographies of
Working Men

Grant Allen

CONTENTS.

BIOGRAPHIES OF WORKING MEN

by

GRANT ALLEN, B.A.

1884

PREFACE.

My acknowledgments are due to Dr. Smiles's "Lives of the Engineers," "Life of the Stephensons," and "Life of a Scotch Naturalist;" to Lady Eastlake's "Life of Gibson;" to Mr. Holden's "Life of Sir William Herschel;" to M. Seusier's "J. F. Millet, Sa Vie et Ses Oeuvres;" and to Mr. Thayer's "Life of President Garfield;" from which most of the facts here narrated have been derived.

G.A.

I.

THOMAS TELFORD, STONEMASON.

High up among the heather-clad hills which form the broad dividing barrier between England and Scotland, the little river Esk brawls and bickers over its stony bed through a wild land of barren braesides and brown peat mosses, forming altogether some of the gloomiest and most forbidding scenery in the whole expanse of northern Britain. Almost the entire bulk of the counties of Dumfries, Kirkcudbright, and Ayr is composed of just such solemn desolate upland wolds, with only a few stray farms or solitary cottages sprinkled at wide distances over their bare bleak surface, and with scarcely any sign of life in any part save the little villages which cluster here and there at long intervals around some stern and simple Scottish church. Yet the hardy people who inhabit this wild and chilly moorland country may well be considered to rank among the best raw material of society in the whole of Britain; for from the peasant homes of these southern Scotch Highlands have come forth, among a host of scarcely less distinguished natives, three men, at least, who deserve to take their place in the very front line of British thinkers or workers—Thomas Telford, Robert Burns, and Thomas Carlyle. By origin, all three alike belonged in the very strictest sense to the working classes; and the story of each is full of lessons or of warnings for every one of us: but that of Telford is perhaps the most encouraging and the most remarkable of all, as showing how much may be accomplished by energy and perseverance, even under the most absolutely adverse and difficult circumstances.

Near the upper end of Eskdale, in the tiny village of Westerkirk, a young shepherd's wife gave birth to a son on the 9th of August, 1757. Her husband, John Telford, was employed in tending sheep on a neighbouring farm, and he and his Janet occupied a small cottage close by, with mud walls and rudely thatched roof, such as in southern England even the humblest agricultural labourer would scarcely consent willingly to inhabit. Before the child was three months old, his father died; and Janet Telford was left alone in the world with her unweaned baby. But in remote country districts, neighbours are often more neighbourly than in great towns; and a poor widow can manage to eke out a livelihood for herself with an occasional lift from the helping hands of friendly fellow- villagers. Janet Telford had nothing to live upon save her own ten fingers; but they were handy enough, after the sturdy Scotch fashion, and they

1

earned some sort of livelihood in a humble way for herself and her fatherless boy. The farmers about found her work on their farms at haymaking or milking, and their wives took the child home with them while its mother was busy labouring in the harvest fields. Amid such small beginnings did the greatest of English engineers before the railway era receive his first hard lessons in the art of life.

After her husband's death, the poor widow removed from her old cottage to a still more tiny hut, which she shared with a neighbour— a very small hut, with a single door for both families; and here young Tam Telford spent most of his boyhood in the quiet honourable poverty of the uncomplaining rural poor. As soon as he was big enough to herd sheep, he was turned out upon the hillside in summer like any other ragged country laddie, and in winter he tended cows, receiving for wages only his food and money enough to cover the cost of his scanty clothing. He went to school, too; how, nobody now knows: but he DID go, to the parish school of Westerkirk, and there he learnt with a will, in the winter months, though he had to spend the summer on the more profitable task of working in the fields. To a steady earnest boy like young Tam Telford, however, it makes all the difference in the world that he should have been to school, no matter how simply. Those twenty-six letters of the alphabet, once fairly learnt, are the key, after all, to all the book-learning in the whole world. Without them, the shepherd-boy might remain an ignorant, unprogressive shepherd all his life long, even his undeniable native energy using itself up on nothing better than a wattled hurdle or a thatched roof; with them, the path is open before him which led Tam Telford at last to the Menai Bridge And Westminster Abbey.

When Tam had gradually eaten his way through enough thin oatmeal porridge (with very little milk, we fear) to make him into a hearty lad of fifteen, it began to be high time for him to choose himself a final profession in life, such as he was able. And here already the born tastes of the boy began to show themselves: for he had no liking for the homely shepherd's trade; he felt a natural desire for a chisel and a hammer—the engineer was there already in the grain—and he was accordingly apprenticed to a stonemason in the little town of Lochmaben, beyond the purple hills to eastward. But his master was a hard man; he had small mercy for the raw lad; and after trying to manage with him for a few months, Tam gave it up, took the law into his own hands, and ran away. Probably the provocation was severe, for in after-life Telford always showed himself duly respectful to constituted authority; and we know that petty self-made master-workmen are often apt to be excessively severe to their own hired helpers, and especially to helpless lads or young apprentices. At any rate, Tam wouldn't go back; and in the end, a well-to-do cousin, who had risen to the proud position of steward at the great hall of the parish, succeeded in getting another mason at Langholm, the little capital of Eskdale, to take over the runaway for the remainder of the term of his indentures.

At Langholm, a Scotch country town of the quietest and sleepiest description, Tam Telford passed the next eight years of his uneventful early life, first as an apprentice, and afterwards as a journeyman mason of the humblest type. He had a good mother, and he was a good son. On Saturday nights he generally managed to walk over to the cottage at Westerkirk, and accompany the poor widow to the Sunday services at the parish kirk. As long as she lived, indeed, he never forgot her; and one of the first tasks he set himself when he was out of his indentures was to cut a neat headstone with a simple but beautiful inscription for the grave of that shepherd father whom he had practically never seen. At Langholm, an old maiden lady, Miss Pasley, interested herself kindly in Janet Telford's rising boy. She lent him what of all things the eager lad most needed—books; and the young mason applied himself to them in all his spare moments with the vigorous ardour and perseverance of healthy youth. The books he read were not merely those which bore directly or indirectly upon his own craft: if they had been, Tam Telford might have remained nothing more than a journeyman mason all the days of his life. It is a great mistake, even from the point of view of mere worldly success, for a young man to read or learn only what "pays" in his particular calling; the more he reads and learns, the more will he find that seemingly useless things "pay" in the end, and that what apparently pays least, often really pays most in the long run. This is not the only or the best reason why every man should aim at the highest possible cultivation of his own talents, be they what they may; but it is in itself a very good reason, and it is a sufficient answer for those who would deter us from study of any high kind on the ground that it "does no good." Telford found in after-life that his early acquaintance with sound English literature did do him a great deal of good: it opened and expanded his mind; it trained his intelligence; it stored his brain with images and ideas which were ever after to him a source of unmitigated delight and unalloyed pleasure. He read whenever he had nothing else to do. He read Milton with especial delight; and he also read the verses that his fellow-countryman, Rob Burns, the Ayrshire ploughman, was then just beginning to speak straight to the heart of every aspiring Scotch peasant lad. With these things Tam Telford filled the upper stories of his brain quite as much as with the trade details of his own particular useful handicraft; and the result soon showed that therein Tam Telford had not acted uncannily or unwisely.

Nor did he read only; he wrote too—verses, not very good, nor yet very bad, but well expressed, in fairly well chosen language, and with due regard to the nice laws of metre and of grammar, which is in itself a great point. Writing verse is an occupation at which only very few even among men of literary education ever really succeed; and nine-tenths of published verse is mere mediocre twaddle, quite unworthy of being put into the dignity of print. Yet Telford did well for all that in trying his hand, with but poor result, at this most difficult and dangerous of all the arts. His rhymes were worth nothing as rhymes; but they were worth a great deal as discipline and training: they helped to form the man, and that in itself is always something. Most men who have in them the power to do any great thing pass in early life through a verse- making stage. The verses never come to much; but they leave their stamp behind them; and the man is all the better in the end for having thus taught himself the restraint, the command of language, the careful choice of expressions, the exercise of deliberate pains in composition, which even bad verse-making necessarily implies. It is a common mistake of near-sighted minds to look only at the immediate results of things, without considering their remoter effects. When Tam Telford, stonemason of Langholm, began at twenty-two years of age to pen poetical epistles to Robert Burns, most of his fellow-workmen doubtless thought he was giving himself up to very foolish and nonsensical practices; but he was really helping to educate Thomas Telford, engineer of the Holyhead Road and the Caledonian Canal, for all his future usefulness and greatness.

As soon as Tam was out of his indentures, he began work as a journeyman mason at Langholm on his own account, at the not very magnificent wages of eighteenpence a day. That isn't much; but at any rate it is an independence. Besides building many houses in his own town, Tam made here his first small beginning in the matter of roads and highways, by helping to build a bridge over the Esk at Langholm. He was very proud of his part in this bridge, and to the end of his life he often referred to it as his first serious engineering work. Many of the stones still bear his private mark, hewn with the tool into their solid surface, with honest workmanship which helps to explain his later success. But the young mason was beginning to discover that Eskdale was hardly a wide enough field for his budding ambition. He could carve the most careful headstones; he could cut the most ornamental copings for doors or windows; he could even build a bridge across the roaring flooded Esk; but he wanted to see a little of the great world, and learn how men and masons went about their work in the busy centres of the world's activity. So, like a patriotic Scotchman that he was, he betook himself straight to Edinburgh, tramping it on foot, of course, for railways did not yet exist, and coaches were not for the use of such as young Thomas Telford.

He arrived in the grey old capital of Scotland in the very nick of time. The Old Town, a tangle of narrow alleys and close courtyards, surrounded by tall houses with endless tiers of floors, was just being deserted by the rich and fashionable world for the New Town, which lies beyond a broad valley on the opposite hillside, and contains numerous streets of solid and handsome stone houses, such as are hardly to be found in any other town in Britain, except perhaps Bath and Aberdeen. Edinburgh is always, indeed, an interesting place for an enthusiastic lover of building, be he architect or stonemason; for instead of being built of brick like London and so many other English centres, it is built partly of a fine hard local sandstone and partly of basaltic greenstone; and besides its old churches and palaces, many of the public buildings are particularly striking and beautiful architectural works. But just at the moment when young Telford walked wearily into Edinburgh at the end of his long tramp, there was plenty for a stout strong mason to do in the long straight stone fronts of the rising New Town. For two years, he worked away patiently at his trade in "the grey metropolis of the North;" and he took advantage of the special opportunities the place afforded him to learn drawing, and to make minute sketches in detail of Holyrood Palace, Heriot's Hospital, Roslyn Chapel, and all the other principal old buildings' in which the neighbourhood of the capital is particularly rich. So anxious, indeed, was the young mason to perfect himself by the study of the very best models in his own craft, that when at the end of two years he walked back to revisit his good mother in Eskdale, he took the opportunity of making drawings of Melrose Abbey, the most exquisite and graceful building that the artistic stone-cutters of the Middle Ages have handed down to our time in all Scotland.

This visit to Eskdale was really Telford's last farewell to his old home, before setting out on a journey which was to form the turning-point in his own history, and in the history of British engineering as well. In Scotch phrase, he was going south. And after taking leave of his mother (not quite for the last time) he went south in good earnest, doing this journey on horseback; for his cousin the steward had lent him a horse to make his way southward like a gentleman. Telford turned where all enterprising young Scotchmen of his time always turned: towards the unknown world of London—that world teeming with so many possibilities of brilliant success or of miserable squalid failure. It was the year 1782, and the young man was just twenty-five. No sooner had he reached the great city than he began looking about him for suitable work. He had a letter of introduction to the architect of Somerset House, whose ornamental fronts were just then being erected, facing the Strand and the river; and Telford was able to get a place at once on the job as a hewer of the finer architectural details, for which both his taste and experience well fitted him. He spent some two years in London at this humble post as a stone-cutter; but already he began to aspire to something better. He earned first- class mason's wages now, and saved whatever he did not need for daily expenses. In this respect, the improvidence of his English fellow-workmen struck the cautious young Scotchman very greatly. They lived, he said, from week to week entirely; any time beyond a week seemed unfortunately to lie altogether outside the range of their limited comprehension.

At the end of two years in London, Telford's skill and study began to bear good fruit. His next engagement was one which raised him for the first time in his life above the rank of a mere journeyman mason. The honest workman had attracted the attention of competent judges. He obtained employment as foreman of works of some important buildings in Portsmouth Dockyard. A proud man indeed was Thomas Telford at this change of fortune, and very proudly he wrote to his old friends in Eskdale, with almost boyish delight, about the trust reposed in him by the commissioners and officers, and the pains he was taking with the task entrusted to him. For he was above all things a good workman, and like all good workmen he felt a pride and an interest in all the jobs he took in hand. His sense of responsibility and his sensitiveness, indeed, were almost too great at times for his own personal comfort. Things WILL go wrong now and then, even with the greatest care; well-planned undertakings will not always pay, and the best engineering does not necessarily succeed in earning a dividend; but whenever such mishaps occurred to his employers, Telford felt the disappointment much too keenly, as though he himself had been to blame for their miscalculations or over-sanguine hopes. Still, it is a good thing to put one's heart in one's work, and so much Thomas Telford certainly did.

About this time, too, the rising young mason began to feel that he must get a little more accurate scientific knowledge. The period for general study had now passed by, and the period for special trade reading had set in. This was well. A lad cannot do better than lay a good foundation of general knowledge and general literature during the period when he is engaged in forming his mind: a young man once fairly launched in life may safely confine himself for a time to the studies that bear directly upon his own special chosen subject. The thing that Telford began closely to investigate was—lime. Now, lime makes mortar; and without lime, accordingly, you can have no mason. But to know anything really about lime, Telford found he must read some chemistry; and to know anything really about chemistry he must work at it hard and unremittingly. A strict attention to one's own business, understood in this very broad and liberal manner, is certainly no bad thing for any struggling handicraftsman, whatever his trade or profession may happen to be.

In 1786, when Telford was nearly thirty, a piece of unexpected good luck fell to his lot. And yet it was not so much good luck as due recognition of his sterling qualities by a wealthy and appreciative person. Long before, while he was still in Eskdale, one Mr. Pulteney, a man of social importance, who had a large house in the bleak northern valley, had asked his advice about the repairs of his own mansion. We may be sure that Telford did his work on that occasion carefully and well; for now, when Mr. Pulteney wished to restore the ruins of Shrewsbury Castle as a dwelling-house, he sought out the young mason who had attended to his Scotch property, and asked him to superintend the proposed alterations in his Shropshire castle. Nor was that all: by Mr. Pulteney's influence, Telford was shortly afterwards appointed to be county surveyor of public works, having under his care all the roads, bridges, gaols, and public buildings in the whole of Shropshire. Thus the Eskdale shepherd-boy rose at last from the rank of a working mason, and attained the well-earned dignity of an engineer and a professional man.

Telford had now a fair opportunity of showing the real stuff of which he was made. Those, of course, were the days when railroads had not yet been dreamt of; when even roads were few and bad;

when communications generally were still in a very disorderly and unorganized condition. It is Telford's special glory that he reformed and altered this whole state of things; he reduced the roads of half Britain to system and order; he made the finest highways and bridges then ever constructed; and by his magnificent engineering works, especially his aqueducts, he paved the way unconsciously but surely for the future railways. If it had not been for such great undertakings as Telford's Holyhead Road, which familiarized men's minds with costly engineering operations, it is probable that projectors would long have stood aghast at the alarming expense of a nearly level iron road running through tall hills and over broad rivers the whole way from London to Manchester.

At first, Telford's work as county surveyor lay mostly in very small things indeed — mere repairs of sidepaths or bridges, which gave him little opportunity to develop his full talents as a born engineer. But in time, being found faithful in small things, his employers, the county magistrates, began to consult him more and more on matters of comparative importance. First, it was a bridge to be built across the Severn; then a church to be planned at Shrewsbury, and next, a second church in Coalbrookdale. If he was thus to be made suddenly into an architect, Telford thought, almost without being consulted in the matter, he must certainly set out to study architecture. So, with characteristic vigour, he went to work to visit London, Worcester, Gloucester, Bath, and Oxford, at each place taking care to learn whatever was to be learned in the practice of his new art. Fortunately, however, for Telford and for England, it was not architecture in the strict sense that he was finally to practise as a real profession. Another accident, as thoughtless people might call it, led him to adopt engineering in the end as the path in life he elected to follow. In 1793, he was appointed engineer to the projected Ellesmere Canal.

In the days before railways, such a canal as this was an engineering work of the very first importance. It was to connect the Mersey, the Dee, and the Severn, and it passed over ground which rendered necessary some immense aqueducts on a scale never before attempted by British engineers. Even in our own time, every traveller by the Great Western line between Chester and Shrewsbury must have observed on his right two magnificent ranges as high arches, which are as noticeable now as ever for their boldness, their magnitude, and their exquisite construction. The first of these mighty archways is the Pont Cysylltau aqueduct which carries the

Ellesmere Canal across the wide valley of the Dee, known as the Vale of Llangollen; the second is the Chirk aqueduct, which takes it over the lesser glen of a minor tributary, the Ceriog. Both these beautiful works were designed and carried out entirely by Telford. They differ from many other great modern engineering achievements in the fact that, instead of spoiling the lovely mountain scenery into whose midst they have been thrown, they actually harmonize with it and heighten its natural beauty. Both works, however, are splendid feats, regarded merely as efforts of practical skill; and the larger one is particularly memorable for the peculiarity that the trough for the water and the elegant parapet at the side are both entirely composed of iron. Nowadays, of course, there would be nothing remarkable in the use of such a material for such a purpose; but Telford was the first engineer to see the value of iron in this respect, and the Pont Cysylltau aqueduct was one of the earliest works in which he applied the new material to these unwonted uses. Such a step is all the more remarkable, because Telford's own education had lain entirely in what may fairly be called the "stone age" of English engineering; while his natural predilections as a stonemason might certainly have made him rather overlook the value of the novel material. But Telford was a man who could rise superior to such little accidents of habit or training; and as a matter of fact there is no other engineer to whom the rise of the present "iron age" in engineering work is more directly and immediately to be attributed than to himself.

Meanwhile, the Eskdale pioneer did not forget his mother. For years he had constantly written to her, in PRINT HAND, so that the letters might be more easily read by her aged eyes; he had sent her money in full proportion to his means; and he had taken every possible care to let her declining years be as comfortable as his altered circumstances could readily make them. And now, in the midst of this great and responsible work, he found time to "run down" to Eskdale (very different "running down" from that which we ourselves can do by the London and North Western Railway), to see his aged mother once more before she died. What a meeting that must have been, between the poor old widow of the Eskdale shepherd, and her successful son, the county surveyor of Shropshire, and engineer of the great and important Ellesmere Canal!

While Telford was working busily upon his wonderful canal, he had many other schemes to carry out of hardly less importance, in connection with his appointment as county surveyor. His beautiful iron bridge across the Severn at Buildwas was another application of his favourite metal to the needs of the new world that was gradually growing up in industrial England; and so satisfied was he with the result of his experiment (for though not absolutely the first, it was one of the first iron bridges ever built) that he proposed another magnificent idea, which unfortunately was never carried into execution. Old London Bridge had begun to get a trifle shaky; and instead of rebuilding it, Telford wished to span the whole river by a single iron arch, whose splendid dimensions would have formed one of the most remarkable engineering triumphs ever invented. The scheme, for some good reason, doubtless, was not adopted; but it is impossible to look at Telford's grand drawing of the proposed bridge—a single bold arch, curving across the Thames from side to side, with the dome of St. Paul's rising majestically above it— without a feeling of regret that such a noble piece of theoretical architecture was never realized in actual fact.

Telford had now come to be regarded as the great practical authority upon all that concerned roads or communications; and he was reaping the due money-reward of his diligence and skill. Every day he was called upon to design new bridges and other important structures in all parts of the kingdom, but more especially in Scotland and on the Welsh border. Many of the most picturesque bridges in Britain, which every tourist has admired, often without inquiring or thinking of the hand that planned them, were designed by his inventive brain. The exquisite stone arch which links the two banks of the lesser Scotch Dee in its gorge at Tongueland is one of the most picturesque; for Telford was a bit of an artist at heart, and, unlike too many modern railway constructors, he always endeavoured to make his bridges and aqueducts beautify rather than spoil the scenery in whose midst they stood. Especially was he called in to lay out the great system of roads by which the Scotch Highlands, then so lately reclaimed from a state of comparative barbarism, were laid open for the great development they have since undergone. In the earlier part of the century, it is true, a few central highways had been run through the very heart of that great solid block of mountains; but these were purely military roads, to enable the king's soldiers more easily to march against the revolted clans, and they had hardly more connection with the life of the country than the bare military posts, like Fort William and Fort Augustus, which guarded their ends, had to do with the ordinary life of a commercial town. Meanwhile, however, the Highlands had begun gradually to settle down; and Telford's roads were intended for the far higher and better purpose of opening out the interior of northern Scotland to the humanizing influences of trade and industry.

Fully to describe the great work which the mature engineer constructed in the Highland region, would take up more space than could be allotted to such a subject anywhere save in a complete industrial history of roads and travelling in modern Britain. It must suffice to say that when Telford took the matter in hand, the vast block of country north and west of the Great Glen of Caledonia (which divides the Highlands in two between Inverness and Ben Nevis)—a block comprising the counties of Caithness, Sutherland, Ross, Cromarty, and half Inverness—had literally nothing within it worthy of being called a road. Wheeled carts or carriages were almost unknown, and all burdens were conveyed on pack-horses, or, worse still, on the broad backs of Highland lassies. The people lived in small scattered villages, and communications from one to another were well-nigh impossible. Telford set to work to give the country, not a road or two, but a main system of roads. First, he bridged the broad river Tay at Dunkeld, so as to allow of a direct route straight into the very jaws of the Highlands. Then, he also bridged over the Beauly at Inverness, so as to connect the opposite sides of the Great Glen with one another. Next, he laid out a number of trunk lines, running through the country on both banks, to the very north of Caithness, and the very west of the Isle of Skye. Whoever to this day travels on the main thoroughfares in the greater Scottish Islands—in Arran, Islay, Jura, Mull; or in the wild peninsula of Morvern, and the Land of Lorne; or through the rugged regions of Inverness-shire and Ross-shire, where the railway has not yet penetrated,—travels throughout on Telford's roads. The number of large bridges and other great engineering masterpieces on this network of roads is enormous; among the most famous and the most beautiful, are the exquisite single arch which spans the Spey just beside the lofty rearing rocks of Craig Ellachie, and the bridge across the Dee, beneath the purple heather-clad braes of Ballater. Altogether, on Telford's Highland roads alone, there are no fewer than twelve hundred bridges.

Nor were these the only important labours by which Telford ministered to the comfort and well-being of his Scotch fellow-countrymen. Scotland's debt to the Eskdale stonemason is indeed deep and lasting. While on land, he improved her communications by his great lines of roads, which did on a smaller scale for the Highland valleys what railways have since done for the whole of the civilized world; he also laboured to improve her means of transit at sea by constructing a series of harbours along that bare and inhospitable eastern coast, once almost a desert, but now teeming with great towns and prosperous industries. It was Telford who formed the harbour of Wick, which has since grown from a miserable fishing village into a large town, the capital of the North Sea herring fisheries. It was he who enlarged the petty port of Peterhead into the chief station of the flourishing whaling trade. It was he who secured prosperity for Fraserburgh, and Banff, and many other less important centres; while even Dundee and Aberdeen, the chief commercial cities of the east coast, owe to him a large part of their present extraordinary wealth and industry. When one thinks how large a number of human beings have been benefited by Telford's Scotch harbour works alone, it is impossible not to envy a great engineer his almost unlimited power of permanent usefulness to unborn thousands of his fellow-creatures.

As a canal-maker, Telford was hardly less successful than as a constructor of roads and harbours. It is true, his greatest work in this direction was in one sense a failure. He was employed by Government for many years as the engineer of the Caledonian Canal, which runs up the Great Glen of Caledonia, connecting the line of lakes whose basins occupy that deep hollow in the Highland ranges, and so avoiding the difficult and dangerous sea voyage round the stormy northern capes of Caithness. Unfortunately, though the canal as an engineering work proved to be of the most successful character, it has never succeeded as a commercial undertaking. It was built just at the exact moment when steamboats were on the point of revolutionizing ocean traffic; and so, though in itself a magnificent and lordly undertaking, it failed to satisfy the sanguine hopes of its projectors. But though Telford felt most bitterly the unavoidable ill success of this great scheme, he might well have comforted himself by the good results of his canal- building elsewhere. He went to Sweden to lay out the Gotha Canal, which still forms the main high-road of commerce between Stockholm and the sea; while in England itself some of his works in this direction—such as the improvements on the Birmingham Canal, with its immense tunnel—may fairly be considered as the direct precursors of the great railway efforts of the succeeding generation.

The most remarkable of all Telford's designs, however, and the one which most immediately paved the way for the railway system, was his magnificent Holyhead Road. This wonderful highway he carried through the very midst of the Welsh mountains, at a comparatively level height for its whole distance, in order to form a main road from London to Ireland. On this road occurs Telford's masterpiece of engineering, the Menai suspension bridge, long regarded as one of the wonders of the world, and still one of the most beautiful suspension bridges in all Europe. Hardly less admirable, however, in its own way is the other suspension bridge which he erected at Conway, to carry his road across the mouth of the estuary, beside the grey old castle, with which its charming design harmonizes so well. Even now it is impossible to drive or walk along this famous and picturesque highway without being struck at every turn by the splendid engineering triumphs which it displays throughout its entire length. The contrast, indeed, between the noble grandeur of Telford's bridges, and the works on the neighbouring railways, is by no means flattering in every respect to our too exclusively practical modern civilization.

Telford was now growing an old man. The Menai bridge was begun in 1819 and finished in 1826, when he was sixty-eight years of age; and though he still continued to practise his profession, and to design many valuable bridges, drainage cuts, and other small jobs, that great undertaking was the last masterpiece of his long and useful life. His later days were passed in deserved honour and comparative opulence; for though never an avaricious man, and always anxious to rate his services at their lowest worth, he had gathered together a considerable fortune by the way, almost without seeking it. To the last, his happy cheerful disposition enabled him to go on labouring at the numerous schemes by which he hoped to benefit the world of workers; and so much cheerfulness was surely well earned by a man who could himself look back upon so good a record of work done for the welfare of humanity. At last, on the 2nd of September, 1834, his quiet and valuable life came gently to a close, in the seventy-eighth year of his age. He was buried in Westminster Abbey, and few of the men who sleep within that great national temple more richly deserve the honour than the Westerkirk shepherd-boy. For Thomas Telford's life was not merely one of worldly success; it was still more pre-eminently one of noble ends and public usefulness. Many working men have raised themselves by their own exertions to a position of wealth and dignity far surpassing his; few indeed have conferred so many benefits upon untold thousands of their fellow-men. It is impossible, even now, to travel in any part of England, Wales, or Scotland, without coming across innumerable memorials of Telford's great and useful life;

impossible to read the full record of his labours without finding that numberless structures we have long admired for their beauty or utility, owe their origin to the honourable, upright, hardworking, thorough-going, journeyman mason of the quiet little Eskdale village. Whether we go into the drained fens of Lincolnshire, or traverse the broad roads of the rugged Snowdon region; whether we turn to St. Katharine's Docks in London, or to the wide quays of Dundee and those of Aberdeen; whether we sail beneath the Menai suspension bridge at Bangor, or drive over the lofty arches that rise sheer from the precipitous river gorge at Cartland, we meet everywhere the lasting traces of that inventive and ingenious brain. And yet, what lad could ever have started in the world under apparently more hopeless circumstances than widow Janet Telford's penniless orphan shepherd-boy Tam, in the bleakest and most remote of all the lonely border valleys of southern Scotland?

II.

GEORGE STEPHENSON, ENGINE-MAN.

Any time about the year 1786, a stranger in the streets of the grimy colliery village of Wylam, near Newcastle, might have passed by without notice a ragged, barefooted, chubby child of five years old, Geordie Stephenson by name, playing merrily in the gutter and looking to the outward eye in no way different from any of the other colliers' children who loitered about him. Nevertheless, that ragged boy was yet destined in after-life to alter the whole face of England and the world by those wonderful railways, which he more than any other man was instrumental in first constructing; and the story of his life may rank perhaps as one of the most marvellous in the whole marvellous history of able and successful British working men.

George Stephenson was born in June, 1781, the son of a fireman who tended the pumping engine of the neighbouring colliery, and one of a penniless family of six children. So poor was his father, indeed, that the whole household lived in a single room, with bare floor and mud wall; and little Geordie grew up in his own unkempt fashion without any schooling whatever, not even knowing A from B when he was a big lad of seventeen. At an age when he ought to have been learning his letters, he was bird's-nesting in the fields or running errands to the Wylam shops; and as soon as he was old enough to earn a few pence by light work, he was set to tend cows at the magnificent wages of twopence a day, in the village of Dewley Burn, close by, to which his father had then removed. It might have seemed at first as though the future railway engineer was going to settle down quietly to the useful but uneventful life of an agricultural labourer; for from tending cows he proceeded in due time (with a splendid advance of twopence) to leading the horses at the plough, spudding thistles, and hoeing turnips on his employer's farm. But the native bent of a powerful mind usually shows itself very early; and even during the days when Geordie was still stumbling across the freshly ploughed clods or driving the cows to pasture with a bunch of hazel twigs, his taste for mechanics already made itself felt in a very marked and practical fashion. During all his leisure time, the future engineer and his chum Bill Thirlwall occupied themselves with making clay models of engines, and fitting up a winding machine with corks and twine like those which lifted the colliery baskets. Though Geordie Stephenson didn't go to school at the village teacher's, he was teaching himself in his own way by close observation and keen comprehension of all the machines and engines he could come across.

Naturally, to such a boy, the great ambition of his life was to be released from the hoeing and spudding, and set to work at his father's colliery. Great was Geordie's joy, therefore, when at last he was taken on there in the capacity of a coal-picker, to clear the loads from stones and rubbish. It wasn't a very dignified position, to be sure, but it was the first step that led the way to the construction of the Liverpool and Manchester Railway. Geordie was now fairly free from the uncongenial drudgery of farm life, and able to follow his own inclinations in the direction of mechanical labour. Besides, was he not earning the grand sum of sixpence a day as picker, increased to eightpence a little later on, when he rose to the more responsible and serious work of driving the gin-horse? A proud day indeed it was for him when, at fourteen, he was finally permitted to aid his father in firing the colliery engine; though he was still such a very small boy that he used to run away and hide when the owner went his rounds of inspection, for fear he should be thought too little to earn his untold wealth of a shilling a day in such a grown-up occupation. Humbler beginnings were never any man's who lived to become the honoured guest, not of kings and princes only, but of the truly greatest and noblest in the land.

A coal-miner's life is often a very shifting one; for the coal in particular collieries gets worked out from time to time; and he has to remove, accordingly, to fresh quarters, wherever employment happens to be found. This was very much the case with George Stephenson and his family; all of them being obliged to remove several times over during his childish days in search of new openings. Shortly after Geordie had attained to the responsible position of assistant fireman, his father was compelled, by the closing of Dewley Burn mine, to get a fresh situation hard by at Newburn. George accompanied him, and found employment as full fireman at a small working, whose little engine he undertook to manage in partnership with a mate, each of them tending the fire night and day by twelve-hour shifts. Two years later, his wages were raised to twelve shillings a week, a sure mark of his diligent and honest work; so that George was not far wrong in remarking to a fellow-workman at the time that he now considered himself a made man for life.

During all this time, George Stephenson never for a moment ceased to study and endeavour to understand the working of every part in the engine that he tended. He was not satisfied, as too many workmen are, with merely learning the routine work of his own trade; with merely knowing that he must turn such and such a tap or valve in order to produce such and such a desired result: he wanted to see for himself how and why the engine did this or that, what was the use and object of piston and cylinder and crank and joint and condenser—in short, fully to understand the underlying principle of its construction. He took it to pieces for cleaning whenever it was needful; he made working models of it after his old childish pattern; he even ventured to tinker it up when out of order on his own responsibility. Thus he learnt at last something of the theory of the steam-engine, and learnt also by the way a great deal about the general principles of mechanical science. Still, even now, incredible as it seems, the future father of railways couldn't yet read; and he found this terrible drawback told fatally against his further progress. Whenever he wanted to learn something that he didn't quite understand, he was always referred for information to a Book. Oh, those books; those mysterious, unattainable, incomprehensible books; how they must have bothered and worried poor intelligent and aspiring but still painfully ignorant young George Stephenson! Though he was already trying singularly valuable experiments in his own way, he hadn't yet even begun to learn his letters.

Under these circumstances, George Stephenson, eager and anxious for further knowledge, took a really heroic resolution. He wasn't ashamed to go to school. Though now a full workman on his own account, about eighteen years old, he began to attend the night school at the neighbouring village of Walbottle, where he took lessons in reading three evenings every week. It is a great thing when a man is not ashamed to learn. Many men are; they consider themselves so immensely wise that they look upon it as an impertinence in anybody to try to tell them anything they don't know already. Truly wise or truly great men—men with the capability in them for doing anything worthy in their generation—never feel this false and foolish shame. They know that most other people know some things in some directions which they do not, and they are glad to be instructed in them whenever opportunity offers. This wisdom George Stephenson possessed in sufficient degree to make him feel more ashamed of his ignorance than of the steps necessary in order to conquer it. Being a diligent and willing scholar, he soon learnt to read, and by the time he was nineteen he had learnt how to write also. At arithmetic, a science closely allied to his native mechanical bent, he was particularly apt, and beat all the other scholars at the village night school. This resolute effort at education was the real turning-point in George Stephenson's remarkable career, the first step on the ladder whose topmost rung led him so high that he himself must almost have felt giddy at the unwonted elevation.

Shortly after, young Stephenson gained yet another promotion in being raised to the rank of brakesman, whose duty it was to slacken the engine when the full baskets of coal reached the top of the shaft. This was a more serious and responsible post than any he had yet filled, and one for which only the best and steadiest workmen were ever selected. His wages now amounted to a pound a week, a very large sum in those days for a skilled working-man.

Meanwhile, George, like most other young men, had fallen in love. His sweetheart, Fanny Henderson, was servant at the small farmhouse where he had taken lodgings since leaving his father's home; and though but little is known about her (for she unhappily died before George had begun to rise to fame and fortune), what little we do know seems to show that she was in every respect a fitting wife for the active young brakesman, and a fitting mother for his equally celebrated son, Robert Stephenson. Fired by the honourable desire to marry Fanny, with a proper regard for prudence, George set himself to work to learn cobbling in his spare moments; and so successfully did he cobble the worn shoes of his fellow-colliers after working hours, that before long he contrived to save a whole guinea out of his humble earnings. That guinea was the first step towards an enormous fortune; a fortune, too, all accumulated by steady toil and constant useful labour for the ultimate benefit of his fellow-men. To make a fortune is the smallest and least noble of all possible personal ambitions; but to save the first guinea which leads us on at last to independence and modest comfort is indeed an important turning-point in every prudent man's career. Geordie Stephenson was so justly proud of his achievement in this respect that he told a friend in confidence he might now consider himself a rich man.

By the time George was twenty-one, he had saved up enough by constant care to feel that he might safely embark on the sea of housekeeping. He was able to take a small cottage lodging for himself and Fanny, at Willington Quay, near his work at the moment, and to furnish it with the simple comfort which was all that their existing needs demanded. He married Fanny on the 28th of November, 1802; and the young couple proceeded at once to their new home. Here George laboured harder than ever, as became the head of a family. He was no more ashamed of odd jobs than he had been of learning the alphabet. He worked overtime at emptying ballast from ships; he continued to cobble, to cut lasts, and even to try his hand at regular shoemaking; furthermore, he actually acquired the art of mending clocks, a matter which lay strictly in his own line, and he thus earned a tidy penny at odd hours by doctoring all the rusty or wheezy old timepieces of all his neighbours. Nor did he neglect his mechanical education meanwhile for he was always at work upon various devices for inventing a perpetual motion machine. Now, perpetual motion is the most foolish will-o'-the-wisp that ever engaged a sane man's attention: the thing has been proved to be impossible from every conceivable point of view, and the attempt to achieve it, if pursued to the last point, can only end in disappointment if not in ruin. Still, for all that, the work George Stephenson spent upon this unpractical object did really help to give him an insight into mechanical science which proved very useful to him at a later date. He didn't discover perpetual motion, but he did invent at last the real means for making the locomotive engine a practical power in the matter of travelling.

A year later, George's only son Robert was born; and from that moment the history of those two able and useful lives is almost inseparable. During the whole of George Stephenson's long upward struggle, and during the hard battle he had afterwards to fight on behalf of his grand design of railways, he met with truer sympathy, appreciation, and comfort from his brave and gifted son than from any other person whatsoever. Unhappily, his pleasure and delight in the up-bringing of his boy was soon to be clouded for a while by the one great bereavement of an otherwise singularly placid and happy existence. Some two years after her marriage, Fanny Stephenson died, as yet a mere girl, leaving her lonely husband to take care of their baby boy alone and unaided. Grief for this irretrievable loss drove the young widower away for a while from his accustomed field of work among the Tyneside coal-pits; he accepted an invitation to go to Montrose in Scotland, to overlook the working of a large engine in some important spinning-works. He remained in this situation for one year only; but during that time he managed to give clear evidence of his native mechanical insight by curing a defect in the pumps which supplied water to his engine, and which had hitherto defied the best endeavours of the local engineers. The young father was not unmindful, either, of his duty to his boy, whom he had left behind with his grandfather on Tyneside; for he saved so large a sum as 28 pounds during his engagement, which he carried back with him in his pocket on his return to England.

A sad disappointment awaited him when at last he arrived at home. Old Robert Stephenson, the father, had met with an accident during George's absence which made him quite blind, and incapacitated him for further work. Helpless and poor, he had no resource to save him from the workhouse except George; but George acted towards him exactly as all men who have in them a possibility of any good thing always do act under similar circumstances. He spent 15 pounds of his hard-earned savings to pay the debts the poor blind old engine- man had necessarily contracted during his absence, and he took a comfortable cottage for his father and mother at Killingworth, where he had worked before his removal to Scotland, and where he now once more obtained employment, still as a brakesman. In that cottage this good and brave son supported his aged parents till their death, in all the simple luxury that his small means would then permit him.

That, however, was not the end of George's misfortunes. Shortly after, he was drawn by lot as a militiaman; and according to the law of that time (for this was in 1807, during the very height of the wars against Napoleon) he must either serve in person or else pay heavily to secure a substitute. George chose regretfully the latter course—the only one open to him if he wished still to support his parents and his infant son. But in order to do so, he had to pay away the whole remainder of his carefully hoarded savings, and even to borrow 6 pounds to make up the payment for the substitute. It must have seemed very hard to him to do this, and many men would have sunk under the blow, become hopeless, or taken to careless rowdy drinking habits. George Stephenson felt it bitterly, and gave way for a while to a natural despondency; he would hardly have been human if he had not; but still, he lived over it, and in the end worked on again with fuller resolution and vigour than ever.

For several years Geordie, as his fellow-colliers affectionately called him, continued to live on at one or other of the Killingworth collieries. In a short time, he entered into a small contract with his employers for "brakeing" the engines; and in the course of this contract, he invented certain improvements in the matter of saving wear and tear of ropes, which were both profitable to himself and also in some small degree pointed the way toward his future plans for the construction of railways. It is true, the two subjects have not, apparently, much in common; but they are connected in this way, that both proceed upon the principle of reducing the friction to the smallest possible quantity. It was this principle that Stephenson was gradually learning to appreciate more and more at its proper value; and it was this which finally led him to the very summit of a great and pre-eminently useful profession. The great advantage, indeed, of a level railway over an up-and-down ordinary road is simply that in the railway the resistance and friction are almost entirely got rid of.

It was in 1810, when Stephenson was twenty-nine, that his first experiment in serious engineering was made. A coal-pit had been sunk at Killingworth, and a rude steam-engine of that time had been set to pump the water out of its shaft; but, somehow, the engine made no headway against the rising springs at the bottom of the mine. For nearly a year the engine worked away in vain, till at last, one Saturday afternoon, Geordie Stephenson went over to examine her. "Well, George," said a pitman, standing by, "what do you think of her?" "Man," said George, boldly, "I could alter her and make her draw. In a week I could let you all go the bottom." The pitman reported this confident speech of the young brakesman to the manager; and the manager, at his wits' end for a remedy, determined to let this fellow Stephenson try his hand at her. After all, if he did no good, he would be much like all the others; and anyhow he seemed to have confidence in himself, which, if well grounded, is always a good thing.

George's confidence WAS well grounded. It was not the confidence of ignorance, but that of knowledge. He UNDERSTOOD the engine now, and he saw at once the root of the evil. He picked the engine to pieces, altered it to suit the requirements of the case, and set it to work to pump without delay. Sure enough, he kept his word; and within the week, the mine was dry, and the men were sent to the bottom. This was a grand job for George's future. The manager, a Mr. Dodds, not only gave him ten pounds at once as a present, in acknowledgment of his practical skill, but also appointed him engine-man of the new pit, another rise in the social scale as well as in the matter of wages. Dodds kept him in mind for the future, too; and a couple of years later, on a vacancy occurring, he promoted the promising hand to be engine-wright of all the collieries under his management, at a salary of 100 pounds a year. When a man's income comes to be reckoned by the year, rather than by the week or month, it is a sign that he is growing into a person of importance. George had now a horse to ride upon, on his visits of inspection to the various engines; and his work was rather one of mechanical engineering than of mere ordinary labouring handicraft.

The next few years of George Stephenson's life were mainly taken up in providing for the education of his boy Robert. He had been a good son, and he was now a good father. Feeling acutely how much he himself had suffered, and how many years he had been put back, by his own want of a good sound rudimentary education, he determined that Robert should not suffer from a similar cause. Indeed, George Stephenson's splendid abilities were kept in the background far too long, owing to his early want of regular instruction. So the good father worked hard to send his boy to school; not to the village teacher's only, but to a school for gentlemen's sons at Newcastle. By mending clocks and watches in spare moments, and by rigid economy in all unnecessary expenses (especially beer), Stephenson had again gathered together a little hoard, which mounted up this time to a hundred guineas. A hundred guineas is a fortune and a capital to a working man. He was therefore rich enough, not only to send little Robert to school, but even to buy him a donkey, on which the boy made the journey every day from Killingworth to Newcastle. This was in 1815, when George was thirty-four, and Robert twelve. Perhaps no man who ever climbed so high as George Stephenson, had ever reached so little of the way at so comparatively late an age. For in spite of his undoubted success, viewed from the point of view of his origin and early prospects, he was as yet after all nothing more than the common engine-wright of the Killingworth collieries—a long way off as yet from the distinguished father of the railway system.

George Stephenson's connection with the locomotive, however, was even now beginning. Already, in 1816, he and his boy had tried a somewhat higher flight of mechanical and scientific skill than usual, in the construction of a sun-dial, which involves a considerable amount of careful mathematical work; and now George found that the subject of locomotive engines was being forced by circumstances upon his attention. From the moment he was appointed engine-wright of the Killingworth collieries, he began to think about all possible means of hauling coal at cheaper rates from the pit's mouth to the shipping place on the river. For that humble object alone—an object that lay wholly within the line of his own special business—

did the great railway projector set out upon his investigations into the possibilities of the locomotive. Indeed, in its earliest origin, the locomotive was almost entirely connected with coals and mining; its application to passenger traffic on the large scale was quite a later and secondary consideration. It was only by accident, so to speak, that the true capabilities of railways were finally discovered in the actual course of their practical employment.

George Stephenson was not the first person to construct either a locomotive or a tramway. Both were already in use, in more or less rude forms, at several collieries. But he WAS the first person to bring the two to such a pitch of perfection, that what had been at first a mere clumsy mining contrivance, became developed into a smooth and easy iron highway for the rapid and convenient conveyance of goods and passengers over immense distances. Of course, this great invention, like all other great inventions, was not the work of one day or one man. Many previous heads had helped to prepare the way for George Stephenson; and George Stephenson himself had been working at the subject for many years before he even reached the first stage of realized endeavour. As early as 1814 he constructed his first locomotive at Killingworth colliery; it was not until 1822 that he laid the first rail of his first large line, the Stockton and Darlington Railway.

Stephenson's earliest important improvement in the locomotive consisted in his invention of what is called the steam-blast, by which the steam is made to increase the draught of the fire, and so largely add to the effectiveness of the engine. It was this invention that enabled him at last to make the railway into the great carrier of the world, and to begin the greatest social and commercial upheaval that has ever occurred in the whole history of the human race.

Meanwhile, however, George was not entirely occupied with the consideration of his growing engine. He had the clocks and watches to mend; he had Robert's schooling to look after; and he had another practical matter even nearer home than the locomotive on which to exercise his inventive genius. One day, in 1814, the main gallery of the colliery caught fire. Stephenson at once descended into the burning pit, with a chosen band of volunteers, who displayed the usual heroic courage of colliers in going to the rescue of their comrades; and, at the risk of their lives, these brave men bricked up the burning portion, and so, by excluding the air, put out the dangerous fire. Still, even so, several of the workmen had been suffocated, and one of the pitmen asked Geordie in dismay whether nothing could be done to prevent such terrible disasters in future. "The price of coal-mining now," he said, "is pitmen's lives." Stephenson promised to think the matter over; and he did think it over with good effect. The result of his thought was the apparatus still affectionately known to the pitmen as "the Geordie lamp." It is a lamp so constructed that the flame cannot pass out into the air outside, and so cause explosions in the dangerous fire-damp which is always liable to occur abundantly in the galleries of coal mines. By this invention alone George Stephenson's name and memory might have been kept green for ever; for his lamp has been the means of saving thousands of lives from a sudden, a terrible, and a pitiful death. Most accidents that now occur in mines are due to the neglect of ordinary precautions, and to the perverse habit of carrying a naked lighted candle in the hand (contrary to regulations) instead of a carefully guarded safety lamp. Yet so culpably reckless of their own and other men's lives are a large number of people everywhere, that in spite of the most stringent and salutary rules, explosions from this cause (and, therefore, easily avoidable) take place constantly to the present day, though far less frequently than before the invention of the Geordie lamp.

Curiously enough, at the very time when George Stephenson was busy inventing his lamp at Killingworth, Sir Humphrey Davy was working at just the same matter in London; and the two lamps, though a little different in minor points of construction, are practically the same in general principle. Now, Sir Humphrey was then the great fashionable natural philosopher of the day, the favourite of London society, and the popular lecturer of the Royal Institution. His friends thought it a monstrous idea that his splendid life- saving apparatus should have been independently devised by "an engine-wright of Killingworth of the name of Stephenson—a person not even possessing a knowledge of the elements of chemistry." This sounds very odd reading at the present day, when the engine- wright of the name of Stephenson has altered the whole face of the world, while Davy is chiefly remembered as a meritorious and able chemist; but at the time, Stephenson's claim to the invention met with little courtesy from the great public of London, where a meeting was held on purpose to denounce his right to the credit of the invention. What the coal-owners and colliers of the North Country thought about the matter was sufficiently shown by their subscription of 1000 pounds, as a Stephenson testimonial fund. With part of the money, a silver tankard was presented to the deserving engine-wright, while the remainder of the sum was handed over to him in ready cash. A very acceptable present it was, and one which George Stephenson remembered with pride down to his dying day. The Geordie lamp continues in use to the present moment in the Tyneside collieries with excellent effect.

For some years more, Mr. Stephenson (he is now fairly entitled to that respectable prefix) went on still further experimenting on the question of locomotives and railways. He was now beginning to learn that much unnecessary wear and tear arose on the short lines of rail down from the pit's mouths to the loading-places on the river by the inequalities and roughnesses of the joints; and he invented a method of overlapping the rails which quite got over this source of loss—loss of speed, loss of power, and loss of material at once. It was in 1819 that he laid down his first considerable piece of road, the Hetton railway. The owners of a colliery at the village of Hetton, in Durham, determined to replace their waggon road by a locomotive line; and they invited the now locally famous Killingworth engine-wright to act as their engineer. Stephenson gladly undertook the post; and he laid down a railway of eight miles in length, on the larger part of which the trucks were to be drawn by "the iron horse," as people now began to style the altered and improved locomotive. The Hetton railway was opened in 1822, and the assembled crowd were delighted at beholding a single engine draw seventeen loaded trucks after it, at the extraordinary rate of four miles an hour—nearly as fast as a man could walk. Whence it may be gathered that Stephenson's ideas upon the question of speed were still on a very humble scale indeed.

Before the Hetton railway was opened, however, George Stephenson had shown one more proof of his excellence as a father by sending his boy Robert, now nineteen, to Edinburgh University. It was a serious expense for a man who was even now, after all, hardly more than a working man of the superior grade; but George Stephenson was well repaid for the sacrifice he thus made on behalf of his only son. He lived to see him the greatest practical engineer of his own time, and to feel that his success was in large measure due to the wider and more accurate scientific training the lad had received from his Edinburgh teachers.

In 1819 George married again, his second wife being the daughter of a farmer at Black Callerton.

The work which finally secured the position of George Stephenson and of his dearly loved locomotive was the Stockton and Darlington railway. Like all the other early railways, it was originally projected simply as a mineral line. Darlington lies in the centre of a rich inland mining district; but the impossibility of getting the coal carried to the sea by cart or donkey, long prevented the opening up of its immense natural wealth. At last, as early as 1817, Edward Pease and a few other enterprising Darlington Quakers determined to build a line of railway from the mining region to Stockton, on the river Tees, where the coal could be loaded into sea-going ships. It was a very long line, compared to any railway that had yet been constructed; but it was still only to be worked by horse-power—to be, in fact, what we now call a tramway, rather than a railway in the modern sense. However, while the plan was still undecided, George Stephenson, who had heard about the proposed scheme, went over to Darlington one day, and boldly asked to see Mr. Pease. The good Quaker received him kindly, and listened to his arguments in favour of the locomotive. "Come over to Killingworth some day and see my engine at work," said Stephenson, confidently; "and if you do you will never think of horses again." Mr. Pease, with Quaker caution, came and looked. George put the engine through its paces, and showed off its marvellous capabilities to such good effect that Edward Pease was immediately converted. Henceforth, he became a decided advocate of locomotives, and greatly aided by his wealth and influence in securing their final triumph.

Not only that, but Mr. Pease also aided Stephenson in carrying out a design which George had long had upon his mind—the establishment of a regular locomotive factory, where the work of engine-making for this particular purpose might be carried on with all the necessary finish and accuracy. George himself put into the concern his precious 1000 pounds, not one penny of which he had yet touched; while Pease and a friend advanced as much between them. A factory was forthwith started at Newcastle on a small scale, and the hardworking engine-wright found himself now fully advanced to the commercial dignity of Stephenson and Co. With the gradual growth of railways, that humble Newcastle factory grew gradually into one of the largest and wealthiest manufacturing establishments in all England.

Meanwhile, Stephenson was eagerly pushing on the survey of the Stockton and Darlington railway, all the more gladly now that he knew it was to be worked by means of his own adopted child, the beloved locomotive. He worked at his line early and late; he took the sights with the spirit-level with his own eye; he was determined to make it a model railway. It was a long and heavy work, for railway surveying was then a new art, and the appliances were all fresh and experimental; but in the end, Stephenson brought it to a happy conclusion, and struck at once the death-blow of the old road-travelling system. The line was opened successfully in 1825, and the engine started off on the inaugural ceremony with a magnificent train of thirty-eight vehicles. "Such was its velocity," says a newspaper of the day, "that in some parts the speed was frequently twelve miles an hour."

The success of the Stockton and Darlington railway was so immense and unexpected, the number of passengers who went by it was so great, and the quantity of coal carried for shipment so far beyond anything the projectors themselves could have anticipated, that a desire soon began to be felt for similar works in other places. There are no two towns in England which absolutely need a railway communication from one to the other so much as Liverpool and Manchester. The first is the great port of entry for cotton, the second is the great centre of its manufacture. The Bridgewater canal had helped for a time to make up for the want of water communication between those two closely connected towns; but as trade developed, the canal became too small for the demands upon it, and the need for an additional means of intercourse was deeply felt. A committee was formed to build a railway in this busy district, and after a short time George Stephenson was engaged to superintend its construction.

A long and severe fight was fought over the Liverpool and Manchester railway, and it was at first doubtful whether the scheme would ever be carried out. Many great landowners were strongly opposed to it, and tried their best to keep the bill for authorizing it from passing through Parliament. Stephenson himself was compelled to appear in London as a witness before a parliamentary committee, and was closely cross-examined as to the possibilities of his plan. In those days, even after the success of the Stockton and Darlington line, his views about the future of railways were still regarded by most sober persons as ridiculously wild and enthusiastic; while the notion that trains might be made to travel twice as fast as stage-coaches, was scouted as the most palpable and ridiculous delusion. One of the members of the committee pressed Stephenson very hard with questions. "Suppose," he said, "a cow were to get upon the line, and the engine were to come into collision with it; wouldn't that be very awkward, now?" George looked up at him with a merry twinkle of the eye, and answered in his broad North Country dialect, "Oo, ay, very awkward for the COO."

In spite of all Stephenson's earnestness and mother wit, however, Parliament refused to pass the bill (in 1825), and for the moment the engineer's vexation was bitter to behold. He and his friends plucked up heart, however; they were fighting the winning battle against prejudice and obstruction, and they were sure to conquer in the long run. The line was resurveyed by other engineers; the lands of the hostile owners were avoided; the causes of offence were dexterously smoothed down; and after another hard fight, in 1826, the bill authorizing the construction of the Liverpool and Manchester railway was finally passed. The board at once appointed Stephenson engineer for constructing the line, at a salary of 1000 pounds a year. George might now fairly consider himself entitled to the honours of an Esquire.

The line was a difficult one to construct; but George Stephenson set about it with the skill and knowledge acquired during many years of slow experience; and he performed it with distinguished success. He was now forty-four; and he had had more to do with the laying down of rails than any other man then living. The great difficulty of the Liverpool and Manchester line lay in the fact that it had to traverse a vast shaking bog or morass, Chat Moss, which the best engineers had emphatically declared it would be impossible to cross. George Stephenson, however, had a plan for making the impossible possible. He simply floated his line on a broad bottom, like a ship, on the top of the quaking quagmire; and proceeded to lay down his rails on this seemingly fragile support without further scruple. It answered admirably, and still answers to the present day. The other works on the railway, especially the cuttings, were such as might well have appalled the boldest heart in those experimental ages of railway enterprise. It is easy enough for us now to undertake tunnelling great hills or filling up wide valleys with long ranges of viaduct, because the thing has been done so often, and the prospect of earning a fair return on the money sunk can be calculated with so high a degree of reasonable probability. But it required no little faith for George Stephenson and his backers to drive a level road, for the first time, through solid rocks and over trembling morasses, the whole way from Liverpool to Manchester. He persevered, however, and in 1830, after four years' toilsome and ceaseless labour, during which he had worked far-harder than the sturdiest navvy on the line, his railway was finally opened for regular traffic.

Before the completion of the railway, George Stephenson had taken part in a great contest for the best locomotive at Liverpool, a prize of 500 pounds having been offered by the company to the successful competitor. Stephenson sent in his improved model, the Rocket, constructed after plans of his own and his son Robert's, and it gained the prize against all its rivals, travelling at what was then considered the incredible rate of 35 miles an hour. It was thus satisfactorily settled that the locomotive was the best power for drawing carriages on railways, and George Stephenson's long battle was thus at last practically won.

The opening of the Liverpool and Manchester railway was an era in the history of the world. From the moment that great undertaking was complete, there could no longer be any doubt about the utility and desirability of railways, and all opposition died away almost at once. New lines began immediately to be laid out, and in an incredibly short time the face of England was scarred by the main trunks in that network of iron roads with which its whole surface is now so closely covered. The enormous development of the railway system benefited the Stephenson family in more than one way. Robert Stephenson became the engineer of the vast series of lines now known as the London and North Western; and the increased demand for locomotives caused George Stephenson's small factory at Newcastle to blossom out suddenly into an immense and flourishing manufacturing concern.

The rest of George Stephenson's life is one long story of unbroken success. In 1831, the year after the opening of the Liverpool and Manchester line, George, being now fifty, began to think of settling down in a more permanent home. His son Robert, who was surveying the Leicester and Swannington railway, observed on an estate called Snibston, near Ashby-de-la-Zouch, what to his experienced geological eye looked like the probable indications of coal beneath the surface. He wrote to his father about it, and as the estate was at the time for sale, George, now a comparatively wealthy man, bought it up on his son's recommendation. He also pitched his home close by at Alton Grange, and began to sink shafts in search of coal. He found it in due time; and thus, in addition to his Newcastle works, he became a flourishing colliery proprietor. It is pleasing to note that Stephenson, unlike too many other self-made men, always treated his workmen with the greatest kindness and consideration, erecting admirable cottages for their accommodation, and providing them with church, chapel, and schools for their religious and social education.

While living at Alton Grange, Stephenson was engaged in laying out several new lines in the middle and north of England, especially the Grand Junction and the Midland, both of which he constructed with great boldness and practical skill. As he grew older and more famous, he began to mix in the truly best society of England; his acquaintance being sought by all the most eminent men in literature, science, and political life. Though but an uneducated working man by origin, George Stephenson had so improved his mind by constant thought and expansive self-education, that he was able to meet these able and distinguished friends of his later days on terms of perfect intellectual and social equality. To the last, however, he never forgot his older and poorer friends, nor was he ever ashamed of their acquaintance. A pleasant trait is narrated by his genial biographer, Dr. Smiles, who notices that on one occasion he stopped to speak to one of his wealthy acquaintances in a fine carriage, and then turned to shake hands with the coachman on the box, whom he had known and respected in his earlier days. He enjoyed, too, the rare pleasure of feeling his greatness recognized in his own time: and once, when he went over to Brussels on a visit to the king of the Belgians, he was pleased and surprised, as the royal party entered the ball-room at the Town Hall, to hear a general murmur among the guests of "Which is Stephenson?"

George Stephenson continued to live for sixteen years, first at Alton Grange, and afterwards at Tapton House, near Chesterfield, in comfort and opulence; growing big pines and melons, keeping birds and dogs, and indulging himself towards the end in the well-earned repose to which his useful and laborious life fully entitled him. At last, on the 12th of August, 1848, he died suddenly of intermittent fever, in his sixty-seventh year, and was peacefully buried in Chesterfield church. Probably no one man who ever lived did so much to change and renovate the whole aspect of human life as George Stephenson; and, unlike many other authors of great revolutions, he lived long enough to see the full result of his splendid labours in the girdling of England by his iron roads. A grand and simple man, he worked honestly and steadfastly throughout his days, and he found his reward in the unprecedented benefits which his locomotive was even then conferring upon his fellow-men. It is indeed wonderful to think how very different is the England in which we live to-day, from that in which we might possibly have been living were it not for the barefooted little collier boy who made clay models of engines at Wylam, and who grew at last into the great and famous engineer of the marvellous Liverpool and Manchester railway. The main characteristic of George Stephenson was perseverance; and it was that perseverance that enabled him at last to carry out his magnificent schemes in the face of so much bitter and violent opposition.

III.

JOHN GIBSON, SCULPTOR.

In most cases, the working man who raises himself to wealth and position, does so by means of trade, which is usually the natural outgrowth of his own special handicraft or calling. If he attains, not only to riches, but to distinction as well, it is in general by mechanical talent, the direction of the mind being naturally biased by the course of one's own ordinary occupations. England has been exceptionally rich in great engineers and inventive geniuses of such humble origin—working men who have introduced great improvements in manufactures or communications; and our modern English civilization has been immensely influenced by the lives of these able and successful mechanical toilers. From Brindley, the constructor of the earliest great canal, to Joseph Gillott, the inventor of the very steel pen with which this book is written; from Arkwright the barber who fashioned the first spinning-machine, to Crompton the weaver, whose mule gave rise to the mighty Manchester cotton trade; from Newcomen, who made the first rough attempt at a steam-engine, to Stephenson, who sent the iron horse from end to end of the land,—the chief mechanical improvements in the country have almost all been due to the energy, intelligence, and skill of our labouring population. The English mind is intensely practical, and the English working man, for the last two centuries at least, has been mainly distinguished for his great mechanical aptitude, bursting out, here and there, in exceptional persons, under the form of exceedingly high inventive genius.

At our very doors, however, there is a small nation of largely different blood and of wholly different speech from our own; a nation forming a part of our own kingdom, even more closely than the Scotch or the Irish, and yet in some respects further from us in mind and habit of life than either; a nation marked rather by the poetical and artistic, than by the mechanical and practical temperament—the ancient and noble Welsh people. It would hardly be reasonable to expect from the Welsh exactly the same kind of success in life which we often find in English workmen; the aims and ideals of the two races are so distinct, and it must be frankly confessed the advantage is not always on the side of the Englishman. The Welsh peasants, living among their own romantic hills and valleys, speaking their own soft and exquisite language, treasuring their own plaintive and melodious poetry, have grown up with an intense love for beauty and the beautiful closely intwined into the very warp and woof of their inmost natures. They have almost always a natural refinement of manner and delicacy of speech which is unfortunately too often wanting amongst our rougher English labouring classes, especially in large towns. They are intensely musical, producing a very large proportion of the best English singers and composers. They are fond of literature, for which they have generally some natural capacity, and in which they exercise themselves to an extent unknown, probably, among people of their class in any other country. At the local meetings of bards (as they call themselves) in Wales, it is not at all uncommon to hear that the first prize for Welsh poetry has been carried off by a shepherd, and the first prize for Welsh prose composition by a domestic servant. In short, the susceptibilities of the race run rather toward art and imagination, than toward mere moneymaking and practical ingenuity.

John Gibson, sculptor, of Rome, as he loved to call himself, was a remarkable embodiment, in many ways, of this self-respecting, artistic, ideal Welsh peasant temperament. In a little village near Conway, in North Wales, there lived at the end of the last century a petty labouring market gardener of the name of Gibson, who knew and spoke no other tongue than his native Welsh. In 1790, his wife gave birth to a son whom they christened John, and who grew up, a workman's child, under the shadow of the great castle, and among the exquisite scenery of the placid land-locked Conway river. John Gibson's parents, like the mass of labouring Welsh people, were honest, God-fearing folk, with a great earnestness of principle, a profound love of truth, and a hatred of all mean or dirty actions. They brought up the boy in these respects in the way he should go; and when he was old he indeed did not depart from them. Throughout his life, John Gibson was remarkable for his calm, earnest, straightforward simplicity, a simplicity which seemed almost childish to those who could not understand so grand and uncommon and noble a nature as his.

From his babyhood, almost, the love of art was innate in the boy; and when he was only seven years old, he began to draw upon a slate a scene that particularly pleased him—a line of geese sailing upon the smooth glassy surface of a neighbouring pond. He drew them as an ordinary child almost always does draw—one goose after another, in profile, as though they were in procession, without any attempt at grouping or perspective in any way. His mother praised the first attempt, saying to him in Welsh, "Indeed, Jack, this is very like the geese;" and Jack, encouraged by her praise, decided immediately to try again. But not being an ordinary child, he determined this time to do better; he drew the geese one behind the other as one generally sees them in actual nature. His mother then asked him to draw a horse; and "after gazing long and often upon one," he says, "I at last ventured to commit him to the slate." When he had done so, the good mother was even more delighted. So, to try his childish art, she asked him to put a rider on the horse's back. Jack went out once more, "carefully watched men on horseback," and then returning, made his sketch accordingly. In this childish reminiscence one can see already the first workings of that spirit which made Gibson afterwards into the greatest sculptor of all Europe. He didn't try even then to draw horse or man by mere guesswork; he went out and studied the subject at first hand. There are in that single trait two great elements of success in no matter what line of life—supreme carefulness, and perfect honesty of workmanship.

When Jack was nine years old, his father determined to emigrate to America, and for that purpose went to Liverpool to embark for the United States. But when he had got as far as the docks, Mrs. Gibson, good soul, frightened at the bigness of the ships (a queer cause of alarm), refused plumply ever to put her foot on one of them. So her husband, a dutiful man with a full sense of his wife's government upon him, consented unwillingly to stop in Liverpool, where he settled down to work again as a gardener. Hitherto, Jack and his brothers had spoken nothing but Welsh; but at Liverpool he was put to school, and soon learned to express himself correctly and easily in English. Liverpool was a very different place for young Jack Gibson from Conway: there were no hills and valleys there, to be sure, but there were shops—such shops! all full of the most beautiful and highly coloured prints and caricatures, after the fashion of the days when George IV. was still Prince Regent. All his spare time he now gave up to diligently copying the drawings which he saw spread out in tempting array before him in the shop-windows. Flattening his little nose against the glass panes, he used to look long and patiently at a single figure, till he had got every detail of its execution fixed firmly on his mind's eye; and then he would go home hastily and sketch it out at once while the picture was still quite fresh in his vivid memory. Afterwards he would return to the shop-window, and correct his copy by the original till it was completely finished. No doubt the boy did all this purely for his own amusement; but at the same time he was quite unconsciously teaching himself to draw under a very careful and accurate master—himself. Already, however, he found his paintings had patrons, for he sold them when finished to the other boys; and once he got as much as sixpence for a coloured picture of Napoleon crossing the Alps—"the largest sum," he says brightly in his memoirs long after, "I had yet received for a work of art."

Opportunities always arise for those who know how to use them. Little Jack Gibson used to buy his paper and colours at a stationer's in Liverpool, who one day said to him kindly, "My lad, you're a constant customer here: I suppose you're a painter." "Yes, sir," Jack answered, with childish self-complacency, "I do paint." The stationer, who had himself studied at the Royal Academy, asked him to bring his pictures on view; and when Jack did so, his new friend, Mr. Tourmeau, was so much pleased with them that he lent the boy drawings to copy, and showed him how to draw for himself from plaster casts. These first amateur lessons must have given the direction to all Gibson's later life: for when the time came for him to choose a trade, he was not set to till the ground like his father, but was employed at once on comparatively artistic and intelligent handicraft.

Jack was fourteen when his father apprenticed him to a firm of cabinet-makers. For the first year, he worked away contentedly at legs and mouldings; but as soon as he had learnt the rudiments of the trade he persuaded his masters to change his indentures, and let him take the more suitable employment of carving woodwork for ornamental furniture. He must have been a good workman and a promising boy, one may be sure, or his masters would never have countenanced such a revolutionary proceeding on the part of a raw apprentice. Young Gibson was delighted with his new occupation, and pursued it so eagerly that he carved even during his leisure hours from plaster casts. But after another year, as ill-luck or good fortune would have it, he happened to come across a London marble-cutter, who had come down to Liverpool to carve flowers in marble for a local firm. The boy was enchanted with his freer and more artistic work; when the marble-cutter took him over a big yard, and showed him the process of modelling and cutting, he began to feel a deep contempt for his own stiff and lifeless occupation of woodcarving. Inspired with the desire to learn this higher craft, he bought some clay, took it home, and moulded it for himself after all the casts he could lay his hands on. Mr. Francis, the proprietor of the marble works, had a German workman in his employ of the name of

Luge, who used to model small figures, chiefly, no doubt, for monumental purposes. Young Gibson borrowed a head of Bacchus that Luge had composed, and made a copy of it himself in clay. Mr. Francis was well pleased with this early attempt, and also with a clever head of Mercury in marble, which Gibson carved in his spare moments.

The more the lad saw of clay and marble, the greater grew his distaste for mere woodwork. At last, he determined to ask Mr. Francis to buy out his indentures from the cabinet-makers, and let him finish his apprenticeship as a sculptor. But unfortunately the cabinet-makers found Gibson too useful a person to be got rid of so easily: they said he was the most industrious lad they had ever had; and so his very virtues seemed as it were to turn against him. Not so, really: Mr. Francis thought so well of the boy that he offered the masters 70 pounds to be quit of their bargain; and in the end, Gibson himself having made a very firm stand in the matter, he was released from his indentures and handed over finally to Mr. Francis and a sculptor's life.

And now the eager boy was at last "truly happy." He had to model all day long, and he worked away at it with a will. Shortly after he went to Mr. Francis's yard, a visitor came upon business, a magnificent-looking old man, with snowy hair and Roman features. It was William Roscoe, the great Liverpool banker, himself a poor boy who had risen, and who had found time not only to build up for himself an enormous fortune, but also to become thoroughly well acquainted with literature and art by the way. Mr. Roscoe had written biographies of Lorenzo de Medici, the great Florentine, and of Leo X., the art-loving pope; and throughout his whole life he was always deeply interested in painting and sculpture and everything that related to them. He was a philanthropist, too, who had borne his part bravely in the great struggle for the abolition of the slave trade; and to befriend a struggling lad of genius like John Gibson was the very thing that was nearest and dearest to his benevolent heart. Mr. Francis showed Roscoe the boy's drawings and models; and Roscoe's appreciative eye saw in them at once the visible promise of great things to be. He had come to order a chimney-piece for his library at Allerton, where his important historical works were all composed; and he determined that the clever boy should have a chief hand in its production. A few days later he returned again with a valuable old Italian print. "I want you to make a bas-relief in baked clay," he said to Gibson, "from this print for the centres of my mantelpiece." Gibson was overjoyed. The print was taken from a fresco of Raphael's in the Vatican at Rome, and Gibson's work was to reproduce it in clay in low relief, as a sculpture picture. He did so entirely to his new patron's satisfaction, and this his first serious work is now duly preserved in the Liverpool Institution which Mr. Roscoe had been mainly instrumental in founding.

Roscoe had a splendid collection of prints and drawings at Allerton; and he invited the clever Welsh lad over there frequently, and allowed him to study them all to his heart's content. To a lad like John Gibson, such an opportunity of becoming acquainted with the works of Raphael and Michael Angelo was a great and pure delight. Before he was nineteen, he began to think of a big picture which he hoped to paint some day; and he carried it out as well as he was able in his own self-taught fashion. For as yet, it must be remembered, Gibson had had no regular artistic instruction: there was none such, indeed, to be had at all in Liverpool in his day; and there was no real art going on in the town in any way. Mr. Francis, his master, was no artist; nor was there anybody at the works who could teach him: for as soon as Mr. Francis found out the full measure of Gibson's abilities, he dismissed his German artist Luge, and put the clever boy entirely in his place. At this time, Gibson was only receiving six shillings a week as wages; but Mr. Francis got good prices for many of his works, and was not ashamed even to put his own name upon the promising lad's artistic performances.

Mr. Roscoe did not merely encourage the young sculptor; he set him also on the right road for ultimate success. He urged Gibson to study anatomy, without which no sculpture worthy of the name is possible. Gibson gladly complied, for he knew that Michael Angelo had been a great anatomist, and Michael was just at that moment the budding sculptor's idol and ideal. But how could he learn? A certain Dr. Vose was then giving lectures on anatomy to young surgeons at Liverpool, and on Roscoe's recommendation he kindly admitted the eager student gratis to his dissecting-room. Gibson dissected there with a will in all his spare moments, and as he put his mind into the work he soon became well versed in the construction of the human body.

From the day that Gibson arrived at man's estate, the great dream of his life was to go to Rome. For Rome is to art what London is to industry—the metropolis in its own way of the entire earth. But travelling in 1810 cost a vast deal of money; and the poor Liverpool marble-cutter (for as yet he was really nothing more) could hardly hope to earn the immense sum that such an expedition would necessarily cost him. So for six years more he went on working at Liverpool in his own native untaught fashion, doing his best to perfect himself, but feeling sadly the lack of training and competition. One of the last works he executed while still in Mr. Francis's service was a chimney-piece for Sir John Gladstone, father of the future premier. Sir John was so pleased with the execution, that he gave the young workman ten pounds as a present. But in spite of occasional encouragement like this, Gibson felt himself at Liverpool, as he says, "chained down by the leg, and panting for liberation."

In 1817, when he was just twenty-seven, he determined to set off to London. He took with him good introductions from Mr. Roscoe to Mr. Brougham (afterwards Lord Chancellor), to Christie, the big picture-dealer, and to several other influential people. Later on, Roscoe recommended him to still more important leaders in the world of art—Flaxman the great sculptor, Benjamin West, the Quaker painter and President of the Royal Academy, and others of like magnitude. Mr. Watson Taylor, a wealthy art patron, gave Gibson employment, and was anxious that he should stop in London. But Gibson wanted more than employment; he wanted to LEARN, to perfect himself, to become great in his art. He could do that nowhere but at Rome, and to Rome therefore he was determined to go. Mr. Taylor still begged him to wait a little. "Go to Rome I will," Gibson answered boldly, "even if I have to go there on foot."

He was not quite reduced to this heroic measure, however, for his Liverpool friends made up a purse of 150 pounds for him (we may be sure it was repaid later on); and with that comparatively large sum in his pocket the young stone-cutter started off gaily on his continental tour, from which he was not to return for twenty-seven years. He drove from Paris to Rome, sharing a carriage with a Scotch gentleman; and when he arrived in the Pope's city (as it then was) he knew absolutely not a single word of Italian, or of any other language on earth save Welsh and English. In those days, Canova, the great Venetian sculptor, was the head of artistic society in Rome; and as ALL society in Rome is more or less artistic, he might almost be said to have led the whole life of the great and lively city. Indeed, the position of such a man in Italy resembles far more that of a duke in England than of an artist as we here are accustomed to think of him. Gibson had letters of introduction to this prince of sculptors from his London friends; and when he went to present them, he found Canova in his studio, surrounded by his numerous scholars and admirers. The Liverpool stone-cutter had brought a few of his drawings with him, and Canova examined them with great attention. Instinctively he recognized the touch of genius. When he had looked at them keenly for a few minutes, he turned kindly to the trembling young man, and said at once, "Come to me alone next week, for I want to have a talk with you."

On the appointed day, Gibson, quivering with excitement; presented himself once more at the great master's studio. Canova was surrounded as before by artists and visitors; but in a short time he took Gibson into a room by himself, and began to speak with him in his very broken English. Many artists came to Rome, he said, with very small means, and that perhaps might be Gibson's case. "Let me have the gratification, then," he went on, "of assisting you to prosecute your studies. I am rich. I am anxious to be of use to you. Let me forward you in your art as long as you stay in Rome."

Gibson replied, with many stammerings, that he hoped his slender means would suffice for his personal needs, but that if Canova would only condescend to give him instruction, to make him his pupil, to let him model in his studio, he would be eternally grateful. Canova was one of the most noble and lovable of men. He acceded at once to Gibson's request, and Gibson never forgot his kind and fatherly assistance. "Dear generous master," the Welsh sculptor wrote many years after, when Canova had long passed away, "I see you before me now. I hear your soft Venetian dialect, and your kindly words inspiring my efforts and gently correcting my defects. My heart still swells with grateful recollection of you."

Canova told his new pupil to devote a few days first to seeing the sights of Rome; but Gibson was impatient to begin at once. "I shall be at your studio to-morrow morning," the ardent Welshman said; and he kept his word. Canova, pleased with so much earnestness and promptitude, set him to work forthwith upon a clay model from his own statue of the Pugilist. Gibson went to the task with a will, moulding the clay as best he could into shape; but he still knew so little of the technical ways of regular sculptors that he tried to model this work from the clay alone, though its pose was such that it could not possibly hold together without an iron framework. Canova saw his error and smiled, but let him go on so that he might learn his business by experience. In a day or two the whole thing, of course, collapsed by its own weight; and then Canova called in a blacksmith and showed the eager beginner how the mechanical skeleton was formed with iron bars, and interlacing crosses of wood and wire. This was quite a new idea to Gibson, who had modelled hitherto only in his own self-taught fashion with moist clay, letting it support its own weight as best it might. Another pupil then fleshed out the iron skeleton with clay, and roughly shaped it to the required figure, so that it stood as firm as a rock for Gibson to work upon. The new hand turned to vigorously once more; and, in spite of his seeming rawness, finished the copy so well that Canova admitted him at once to the Academy to model from life. At this Academy Canova himself, who loved art far more than money, used to attend twice a week to give instruction to students without receiving any remuneration whatsoever. It is of such noble men as this that the world of art is largely made up—that world which we too-practical English have always undervalued or even despised.

Gibson's student period at Rome under Canova was a very happy episode in a uniformly happy and beautiful life. His only trouble was that he had not been able to come there earlier. Singularly free from every taint of envy (like all the great sculptors of his time), he could not help regretting when he saw other men turning out work of such great excellence while he was still only a learner. "When I observed the power and experience of youths much younger than myself," he says in his generous appreciative fashion, "their masterly manner of sketching in the figure, and their excellent imitation of nature, my spirits fell many degrees, and I felt humbled and unhappy." He need not have done so, for the man who thus distrusts his own work is always the truest workman; it is only fools or poor creatures who are pleased and self-satisfied with their own first bungling efforts. But the great enjoyment of Rome to Gibson consisted in the free artistic society which he found there. At Liverpool, he had felt almost isolated; there was hardly anybody with whom he could talk on an equality about his artistic interests; nobody but himself cared about the things that pleased and engrossed his earnest soul the most. But at Rome, there was a great society of artists; every man's studio was open to his friends and fellow-workers; and a lively running fire of criticism went on everywhere about all new works completed or in progress. He was fortunate, too, in the exact moment of his residence: Rome then contained at once, besides himself, the two truest sculptors of the present century, Canova the Venetian, and Thorwaldsen the Dane.

Both these great masters were singularly free from jealousy, rivalry, or vanity. In their perfect disinterestedness and simplicity of character they closely resembled Gibson himself. The ardent and pure-minded young Welshman, who kept himself so unspotted from the world in his utter devotion to his chosen art, could not fail to derive an elevated happiness from his daily intercourse with these two noble and sympathetic souls.

After Gibson had been for some time in Canova's studio, his illustrious master told him that the sooner he took to modelling a life-size figure of his own invention, the better. So Gibson hired a studio (with what means he does not tell us in his short sketch of his own life) close to Canova's, so that the great Venetian was able to drop in from time to time and assist him with his criticism and judgment. How delightful is the friendly communion of work implied in all this graceful artistic Roman life! How different from the keen competition and jealous rivalry which too often distinguishes our busy money-getting English existence! In 1819, two years after Gibson's arrival at Rome, he began to model his Mars and Cupid, a more than life-size group, on which he worked patiently and lovingly for many months. When it was nearly finished, one day a knock came at the studio door. After the knock, a handsome young man entered, and announced himself brusquely as the Duke of Devonshire. "Canova sent me," he said, "to see what you were doing." Gibson wasn't much accustomed to dukes in those days—he grew more familiar with them later on—and we may be sure the poor young artist's heart beat a little more fiercely than usual when the stranger asked him the price of his Mars and Cupid in marble. The sculptor had never yet sold a statue, and didn't know how much he ought to ask; but after a few minutes' consideration he said, "Five hundred pounds. But, perhaps," he added timidly, "I have said too much." "Oh no," the duke answered, "not at all too much;" and he forthwith ordered (or, as sculptors prefer to say, commissioned) the statue to be executed for him in marble. Gibson was delighted, and ran over at once to tell Canova, thinking he had done a splendid stroke of business. Canova shared his pleasure, till the young man came to the price; then the older sculptor's face fell ominously. "Five hundred pounds!" he cried in dismay; "why, it won't cover the cost of marble and workmanship." And so indeed it turned out; for when the work was finished, it had stood Gibson in 520 pounds for marble and expenses, and left him twenty pounds out of pocket in the end. So he got less than nothing after all for his many months of thought and labour over clay and marble alike.

Discouraging as this beginning must have proved, it was nevertheless in reality the first important step in a splendid and successful career. It is something to have sold your first statue, even if you sell it at a disadvantage. In 1821 Gibson modelled a group of Pysche and the Zephyrs. That winter Sir George Beaumont, himself a distinguished amateur artist, and a great patron of art, came to Rome; and Canova sent him to see the young Welshman's new composition. Sir George asked the price, and Gibson, this time more cautious, asked for time to prepare an estimate, and finally named 700 pounds. To his joy, Sir George immediately ordered it, and also introduced many wealthy connoisseurs to the rising sculptor's studio. That same winter, also, the Duke of Devonshire came again, and commissioned a bas-relief in marble (which is now at Chatsworth House, with many other of Gibson's works), at a paying price, too, which was a great point for the young man's scanty exchequer.

Unfortunately, Gibson has not left us any notice of how he managed to make both ends meet during this long adult student period at Rome. Information on that point would indeed be very interesting; but so absorbed was the eager Welshman always in his art, that he seldom tells us anything at all about such mere practical every-day matters as bread and butter. To say the truth, he cared but little about them. Probably he had lived in a very simple penurious style during his whole studenthood, taking his meals at a cafe or eating-house, and centering all his affection and ideas upon his beloved studio. But now wealth and fame began to crowd in upon him, almost without the seeking. Visitors to Rome began to frequent the Welshman's rooms, and the death of "the great and good Canova," which occurred in 1822, while depriving Gibson of a dearly loved friend, left him, as it were, that great master's successor. Towards him and Thorwaldsen, indeed, Gibson always cherished a most filial regard. "May I not be proud," he writes long after, "to have known such men, to have conversed with them, watched all their proceedings, heard all their great sentiments on art? Is it not a pleasure to be so deeply in their debt for instruction?" And now the flood of visitors who used to flock to Canova's studio began to transfer their interest to Gibson's. Commission after commission was offered him, and he began to make money faster than he could use it. His life had always been simple and frugal—the life of a working man with high aims and grand ideals: he hardly knew now how to alter it. People who did not understand Gibson used to say in his later days that he loved money, because he made much and spent little. Those who knew him better say rather that he worked much for the love of art, and couldn't find much to do with his money when he had earned it. He was singularly indifferent to gain; he cared not what he eat or drank; he spent little on clothes, and nothing on entertainments; but he paid his workmen liberally or even lavishly; he allowed one of his brothers more than he ever spent upon himself, and he treated the other with uniform kindness and generosity. The fact is, Gibson didn't understand money, and when it poured in upon him in large sums, he simply left it in the hands of friends, who paid him a very small percentage on it, and whom he always regarded as being very kind to take care of the troublesome stuff on his account. In matters of art, Gibson was a great master; in matters of business, he was hardly more than a simple-minded child.

Sometimes queer incidents occurred at Gibson's studio from the curious ignorance of our countrymen generally on the subject of art. One day, a distinguished and wealthy Welsh gentleman called on the sculptor, and said that, as a fellow Welshman, he was anxious to give him a commission. As he spoke, he cast an admiring eye on Gibson's group of Psyche borne by the Winds. Gibson was pleased with his admiration, but rather taken aback when the old gentleman said blandly, "If you were to take away the Psyche and put a dial in the place, it'd make a capital design for a clock." Much later, the first Duke of Wellington called upon him at Rome and ordered a statue of Pandora, in an attitude which he described. Gibson at once saw that the Duke's idea was a bad one, and told him so. By-and-by, on a visit to England, Gibson waited on the duke, and submitted photographs of the work he had modelled. "But, Mr. Gibson," said the old soldier, looking at them curiously, "you haven't followed my idea." "No," answered the sculptor, "I have followed MY OWN." "You are very stubborn," said Wellington. "Duke," answered the sturdy sculptor, "I am a Welshman, and all the world knows that we are a stubborn race." The Iron Duke ought to have been delighted to find another man as unbending as himself, but he wasn't; and in the end he refused the figure, which Gibson sold instead to Lady Marian Alford.

For twenty-seven years Gibson remained at Rome, working assiduously at his art, and rising gradually but surely to the very first place among then living sculptors. His studio now became the great centre of all fashionable visitors to Rome. Still, he made no effort to get rich, though he got rich without wishing it; he worked on merely for art's sake, not for money. He would not do as many sculptors do, keep several copies in marble of his more popular statues for sale; he preferred to devote all his time to new works. "Gibson was always absorbed in one subject," says Lady Eastlake, "and that was the particular work or part of a work—were it but the turn of a corner of drapery—which was then under his modelling hands. Time was nothing to him; he was long and fastidious." His favourite pupil, Miss Hosmer, once expressed regret to him that she had been so long about a piece of work on which she was engaged. "Always try to do the best you can," Gibson answered. "Never mind how long you are upon a work—no. No one will ask how long you have been, except fools. You don't care what fools think."

During his long life at Rome, he was much cheered by the presence and assistance of his younger brother, Mr. Ben, as he always called him, who was also a sculptor, though of far less merit than John Gibson himself. Mr. Ben came to Rome younger than John, and he learned to be a great classical scholar, and to read those Greek and Latin books which John only knew at second hand, but from whose beautiful fanciful stories of gods and heroes he derived all the subjects for his works of statuary. His other brother, Solomon, a strange, wild, odd man, in whom the family genius had degenerated into mere eccentricity, never did anything for his own livelihood, but lived always upon John Gibson's generous bounty. In John's wealthy days, he and Mr. Ben used to escape every summer from the heat and dust of Rome—which is unendurable in July and August—to the delightfully cool air and magnificent mountain scenery of the Tyrol. "I cannot tell you how well I am," he writes on one of these charming visits, "and so is Mr. Ben. Every morning we take our walks in the woods here. I feel as if I were new modelled." Another passage in one of these summer tourist letters well deserves to be copied here, as it shows the artist's point of view of labours like Telford's and Stephenson's. "From Bormio," he says, "the famous road begins which passes over the Stelvio into the Tyrol; the highest carriage-road in the world. We began the ascent early in the morning. It is magnificent and wonderful. Man shows his talents, his power over great difficulties, in the construction of these roads. Behold the cunning little workman—he comes, he explores, and he says, 'Yes, I will send a carriage and horses over these mighty mountains;' and, by Jove, you are drawn up among the eternal snows. I am a great admirer of these roads."

In 1844 Gibson paid his first visit to England, a very different England indeed to the one he had left twenty-seven years earlier. His Liverpool friends, now thoroughly proud of their stone-cutter, insisted upon giving him a public banquet. Glasgow followed the same example; and the simple-minded sculptor, unaccustomed to such honours, hardly knew how to bear his blushes decorously upon him. During this visit, he received a command to execute a statue of the queen. Gibson was at first quite disconcerted at such an awful summons. "I don't know how to behave to queens," he said. "Treat her like a lady," said a friend; and Gibson, following the advice, found it sufficiently answered all the necessities of the situation. But when he went to arrange with the Prince Consort about the statue, he was rather puzzled what he should do about measuring the face, which he always did for portrait sculpture with a pair of compasses. All these difficulties were at last smoothed over; and Gibson was also permitted to drape the queen's statue in Greek costume, for in his artistic conscientiousness he absolutely refused to degrade sculpture by representing women in the fashionable gown of the day, or men in swallow-tail coats and high collars.

Another work which Gibson designed during this visit possesses for us a singular and exceptional interest. It was a statue of George Stephenson, to be erected at Liverpool. Thus, by a curious coincidence, the Liverpool stone-cutter was set to immortalize the features and figure of the Killingworth engine-man. Did those two great men, as they sat together in one room, sculptor and sitter, know one another's early history and strange struggles, we wonder? Perhaps not; but if they did, it must surely have made a bond of union between them. At any rate, Gibson greatly admired Stephenson, just as he had admired the Stelvio road. "I will endeavour to give him a look capable of action and energy," he said; "but he must be contemplative, grave, simple. He is a good subject. I wish to make him look like an Archimedes."

If Gibson admired Stephenson, however, he did not wholly admire Stephenson's railways. The England he had left was the England of mail-coaches. In Italy, he had learnt to travel by carriage, after the fashion of the country; but these new whizzing locomotives, with their time-tables, and their precision, and their inscrutable mysteries of shunts and junctions, were quite too much for his simple, childish, old-world habits. He had a knack of getting out too soon or too late, which often led him into great confusion. Once, when he wanted to go to Chichester, he found himself landed at Portsmouth, and only discovered his mistake when, on asking the way to the cathedral, he was told there was no cathedral in the town at all. Another story of how he tried to reach Wentworth, Lord Fitzwilliam's place, is best told in his own words. "The train soon stopped at a small station, and, seeing some people get out, I also descended; when, in a moment, the train moved on— faster and faster—and left me standing on the platform. I walked a few paces backward and forward in disagreeable meditation. 'I wish to Heaven,' thought I to myself, 'that I was on my way back to Rome with a postboy.' Then I observed a policeman darting his eyes upon me, as if he would look me through. Said I to the fellow, 'Where is that cursed train gone to? It's off with my luggage and here am I.' The man asked me the name of the place where I took my ticket. 'I don't remember,' said I. 'How should I know the name of any of these places?—it's as long as my arm. I've got it written down somewhere.' 'Pray, sir,' said the man, after a little pause, 'are you a foreigner?' 'No,' I replied, 'I am not a foreigner; I'm a sculptor.'"

The consequence of this almost childish carelessness was that Gibson had always to be accompanied on his long journeys either by a friend or a courier. While Mr. Ben lived, he usually took his brother in charge to some extent; and the relation between them was mutual, for while John Gibson found the sculpture, Mr. Ben found the learning, so that Gibson used often to call him "my classical dictionary." In 1847, however, Mr. Ben was taken ill. He got a bad cold, and would have no doctor, take no medicine. "I consider Mr. Ben," his brother writes, "as one of the most amiable of human beings—too good for this world—but he will take no care against colds, and when ill he is a stubborn animal." That summer Gibson went again to England, and when, he came back found Mr. Ben no better. For four years the younger brother lingered on, and in 1851 died suddenly from the effects of a fall in walking. Gibson was thus left quite alone, but for his pupil Miss Hosmer, who became to him more than a daughter.

During his later years Gibson took largely to tinting his statues— colouring them faintly with flesh-tones and other hues like nature; and this practice he advocated with all the strength of his single-minded nature. All visitors to the great Exhibition of 1862 will remember his beautiful tinted Venus, which occupied the place of honour in a light temple erected for the purpose by another distinguished artistic Welshman, Mr. Owen Jones, who did much towards raising the standard of taste in the English people.

In January, 1866, John Gibson had a stroke of paralysis, from which he never recovered. He died within the month, and was buried in the English cemetery at Rome. Both his brothers had died before him; and he left the whole of his considerable fortune to the Royal Academy in England. An immense number of his works are in the possession of the Academy, and are on view there throughout the year.

John Gibson's life is very different in many respects from that of most other great working men whose story is told in this volume. Undoubtedly, he was deficient in several of those rugged and stern qualities to which English working men have oftenest owed their final success. But there was in him a simple grandeur of character, a purity of soul, and an earnestness of aim which raised him at once far above the heads of most among those who would have been the readiest to laugh at and ridicule him. Besides his exquisite taste, his severe love of beauty, and his marvellous power of expressing the highest ideals of pure form, he had one thing which linked him to all the other great men whose lives we have here recounted—his steadfast and unconquerable personal energy. In one sense it may be said that he was not a practical man; and yet in another and higher sense, what could possibly be more practical than this accomplished resolve of the poor Liverpool stone-cutter to overcome all obstacles, to go to, Rome, and to make himself into a great sculptor? It is indeed a pity that in writing for Englishmen of the present day such a life should even seem for a moment to stand in need of a practical apology. For purity, for guilelessness, for exquisite appreciation of the true purpose of sculpture as the highest embodiment of beauty of form, John Gibson's art stands unsurpassed in all the annals of modern statuary.

IV.

WILLIAM HERSCHEL, BANDSMAN.

Old Isaac Herschel, the oboe-player of the King's Guard in Hanover, had served with his regiment for many years in the chilly climate of North Germany, and was left at last broken down in health and spirits by the many hardships of several severe European campaigns. Isaac Herschel was a man of tastes and education above his position; but he had married a person in some respects quite unfitted for him. His good wife, Anna, though an excellent housekeeper and an estimable woman in her way, had never even learned to write; and when the pair finally settled down to old age in Hanover, they were hampered by the cares of a large family of ten children. Respectable poverty in Germany is even more pressing than in England; the decent poor are accustomed to more frugal fare and greater privations than with us; and the domestic life of the Herschel family circle must needs have been of the most careful and penurious description. Still, Isaac Herschel dearly loved his art, and in it he found many amends and consolations for the sordid shifts and troubles of a straitened German household. All his spare time was given to music, and in his later days he was enabled to find sufficient pupils to eke out his little income with comparative comfort.

William Herschel, the great astronomer (born in 1738), was the fourth child of his mother, and with his brothers he was brought up at the garrison school in Hanover, together with the sons of the other common soldiers. There he learned, not only the three R's, but also a little French and English. Still, the boy was not content with these ordinary studies; in his own playtime he took lessons in Latin and mathematics privately with the regimental schoolmaster. The young Herschels, indeed, were exceptionally fortunate in the possession of an excellent and intelligent father, who was able to direct their minds into channels which few people of their position in life have the opportunity of entering. Isaac Herschel was partly of Jewish descent, and he inherited in a marked degree two very striking Jewish gifts — a turn for music, and a turn for philosophy. The Jews are probably the oldest civilized race now remaining on earth; and their musical faculties have been continuously exercised from a time long before the days of David, so that now they produce undoubtedly a far larger proportion of musicians and composers than any other class of the population whatsoever. They are also deeply interested in the same profound theological and philosophical problems which were discussed with so much acuteness and freedom in the Book of Ecclesiastes and the subtle argument of Job and his friends. There has never been a time when the Jewish mind has not exercised itself profoundly on these deep and difficult questions; and the Hanover bandsman inherited from his Jewish ancestry an unusual interest in similar philosophical subjects. Thus, while the little ones were sleeping in the same common room at night, William and his father were often heard discussing the ideas of such abstruse thinkers as Newton and Leibnitz, whose names must have sounded strange indeed to the ordinary frequenters of the Hanover barracks. On such occasions good dame Herschel was often compelled to interpose between them, lest the loudness of their logic should wake the younger children in the crib hard by.

William, however, possessed yet another gift, which he is less likely to have derived from the Jewish side of the house. He and his brother Alexander were both distinguished by a natural taste for mechanics, and early gave proof of their learning by turning neat globes with the equator and ecliptic accurately engraved upon them, or by making model instruments for their own amusement out of bits of pasteboard. Thus, in early opportunities and educational advantages, the young Herschels certainly started in life far better equipped than most working men's sons; and, considering their father's doubtful position, it may seem at first sight rather a stretch of language to describe him as a working man at all. Nevertheless, when one remembers the humble grade of military bandsmen in Germany, even at the present day, and the fact that most of the Herschel family remained in that grade during all their lives, it is clear that William Herschel's life may be fairly included within the scope of the present series. "In my fifteenth year," he says himself, "I enlisted in military service," and he evidently looked upon his enlistment in exactly the same light as that of any ordinary soldier.

England and Hanover were, of course, very closely connected together at the middle of the last century. The king moved about a great deal from one country to the other; and in 1755 the regiment of Hanoverian Guards was ordered on service to England for a year. William Herschel, then seventeen years of age, and already a member of the band, went together with his father; and it was in this modest capacity that he first made acquaintance with the land where he was afterwards to attain the dignity of knighthood and the post of the king's astronomer. He played the oboe, like his father before him, and no doubt underwent the usual severe military discipline of that age of stiff stocks and stern punishments. His pay was very scanty, and out of it he only saved enough to carry home one memento of his English experiences. That memento was in itself a sufficient mark of the stuff from which young Herschel was compounded. It was a copy of "Locke on the Human Understanding." Now, Locke's famous work, oftener named than read, is a very tough and serious bit of philosophical exposition; and a boy of seventeen who buys such a book out of his meagre earnings as a military bandsman is pretty sure not to end his life within the four dismal bare walls of the barrack. It is indeed a curious picture to imagine young William Herschel, among a group of rough and boisterous German soldiers, discussing high mathematical problems with his father, or sitting down quietly in a corner to read "Locke on the Human Understanding."

In 1757, during the Seven Years' War, Herschel was sent with his regiment to serve in the campaign of Rossbach against the French. He was not physically strong, and the hardships of active service told terribly upon the still growing lad. His parents were alarmed at his appearance when he returned, and were very anxious to "remove" him from the service. That, however, was by no means an easy matter for them to accomplish. They had no money to buy his discharge, and so, not to call the transaction by any other than its true name, William Herschel was forced to run away from the army. We must not judge too harshly of this desertion, for the times were hard, and the lives of men in Herschel's position were valued at very little by the constituted authorities. Long after, it is said, when Herschel had distinguished himself by the discovery of the planet Uranus, a pardon for this high military offence was duly handed to him by the king in person on the occasion of his first presentation. George III. was not a particularly wise or brilliant man; but even he had sense enough to perceive that William Herschel could serve the country far better by mapping out the stars of heaven than by playing the oboe to the royal regiment of Hanoverian Guards.

William was nineteen when he ran away. His good mother packed his boxes for him with such necessaries as she could manage, and sent them after him to Hamburg; but, to the boy's intense disgust, she forgot to send the copy of "Locke on the Human Understanding." What a sturdy deserter we have here, to be sure! "She, dear woman," he says plaintively, "knew no other wants than good linen and clothing!" So William Herschel the oboe-player started off alone to earn his living as best he might in the great world of England. It is strange he should have chosen that, of all European countries; for there alone he was liable to be arrested as a deserter: but perhaps his twelvemonth's stay in London may have given him a sense of being at home amongst us which he would have lacked in any other part of Europe. At any rate, hither he came, and for the next three years picked up a livelihood, we know not how, as many other excellent German bandsmen have done before and since him. Our information about his early life is very meagre, and at this period we lose sight of him for a while altogether.

About the year 1760, however, we catch another incidental glimpse of the young musician in his adopted country. By that time, he had found himself once more a regular post as oboist to the Durham militia, then quartered for its muster at Pontefract. A certain Dr. Miller, an organist at Doncaster, was dining one evening at the officers' mess; when his host happened to speak to him in high praise of a young German they had in their band, who was really, he said, a most remarkable and spirited performer. Dr. Miller asked to see (or rather hear) this clever musician; so Herschel was called up, and made to go through a solo for the visitor's gratification. The organist was surprised at his admirable execution, and asked him on what terms he was engaged to the Durham militia. "Only from month to month," Herschel answered. "Then leave them at the end of your month," said Miller, "and come to live with me. I'm a single man; I think we can manage together; and I'm sure I can get you a better situation." Herschel frankly accepted the offer so kindly made, and seems to have lived for much of the next five years with Miller in his little two-roomed cottage at Doncaster. Here he took pupils and performed in the orchestra at public concerts, always in a very quiet and modest fashion. He also lived for part of the time with a Mr. Bulman at Leeds, for whom he afterwards generously provided a place as clerk to the Octagon Chapel at Bath. Indeed, it is a very pleasing trait in William Herschel's character that to the end he was constantly engaged in finding places for his early friends, as well as for the less energetic or less fortunate members of his own family.

During these years, Herschel also seems to have given much attention to the organ, which enabled him to make his next step in life in 1765, when he was appointed organist at Halifax. Now, there is a great social difference between the position of an oboe-player in a band and a church organist; and it was through his organ-playing that Herschel was finally enabled to leave his needy hand-to-mouth life in Yorkshire. A year later, he obtained the post of organist to the

Octagon Chapel at Bath, an engagement which gave him new opportunities of turning his mind to the studies for which he possessed a very marked natural inclination. Bath was in those days not only the most fashionable watering-place in England, but almost the only fashionable watering-place in the whole kingdom. It was, to a certain extent, all that Brighton, Scarborough, Buxton, and Harrogate are to-day, and something more. In our own time, when railways and steamboats have so altered the face of the world, the most wealthy and fashionable English society resorts a great deal to continental pleasure towns like Cannes, Nice, Florence, Vichy, Baden, Ems, and Homburg; but in the eighteenth century it resorted almost exclusively to Bath. The Octagon Chapel was in one sense the centre of life in Bath; and through his connection with it, Herschel was thrown into a far more intelligent and learned society than that which he had left behind him in still rural Yorkshire. New books came early to Bath, and were read and discussed in the reading-rooms; famous men and women came there, and contributed largely to the intellectual life of the place; the theatre was the finest out of London; the Assembly Rooms were famous as the greatest resort of wit and culture in the whole kingdom. Herschel here was far more in his element than in the barracks of Hanover, or in the little two-roomed cottage at rustic Doncaster.

He worked very hard indeed, and his work soon brought him comfort and comparative wealth. Besides his chapel services, and his later engagement in the orchestra of the Assembly Rooms, he had often as many as thirty-eight private pupils in music every week; and he also composed a few pieces, which were published in London with some modest success. Still, in spite of all these numerous occupations, the eager young German found a little leisure time to devote to self-education; so much so that, after a fatiguing day of fourteen or sixteen hours spent in playing the organ and teaching, he would "unbend his mind" by studying the higher mathematics, or give himself a lesson in Greek and Italian. At the same time; he was also working away at a line of study, seemingly useless to him, but in which he was afterwards to earn so great and deserved a reputation. Among the books he read during this Bath period were Smith's "Optics" and Lalande's "Astronomy." Throughout all his own later writings, the influence of these two books, thoroughly mastered by constant study in the intervals of his Bath music lessons, makes itself everywhere distinctly felt.

Meanwhile, the family at Hanover had not been flourishing quite so greatly as the son William was evidently doing in wealthy England. During all those years, the young man had never forgotten to keep up a close correspondence with his people in Germany. Already, in 1764, during his Yorkshire days, William Herschel had managed out of his Savings as an oboe-player to make a short trip to his old home; and his sister Carolina, afterwards his chief assistant in his astronomical labours, notes with pleasure the delight she felt in having her beloved brother with her once more, though she, poor girl, being cook to the household apparently, could only enjoy his society when she was not employed "in the drudgery of the scullery." A year later, when William had returned to England again, and had just received his appointment as organist at Halifax, his father, Isaac, had a stroke of paralysis which ended his violin-playing for ever, and forced him to rely thenceforth upon copying music for a precarious livelihood. In 1767 he died, and poor Carolina saw before her in prospect nothing but a life of that domestic drudgery which she so disliked. "I could not bear the idea of being turned into a housemaid," she says; and she thought that if only she could take a few lessons in music and fancy work she might get "a place as governess in some family where the want of a knowledge of French would be no objection." But, unhappily, good dame Herschel, like many other uneducated and narrow-minded persons, had a strange dread of too much knowledge. She thought that "nothing further was needed," says Carolina, "than to send me two or three months to a sempstress to be taught to make household linen; so all that my father could do was to indulge me sometimes with a short lesson on the violin when my mother was either in good humour or out of the way. It was her certain belief that my brother William would have returned to his country, and my eldest brother would not have looked so high, if they had had a little less learning." Poor, purblind, well-meaning, obstructive old dame Herschel! what a boon to the world that children like yours are sometimes seized with this incomprehensible fancy for "looking too high"!

Nevertheless, Carolina managed by rising early to take a few lessons at daybreak from a young woman whose parents lived in the same cottage with hers; and so she got through a little work before the regular daily business of the family began at seven. Imagine her delight then, just as the difficulties after her father's death are making that housemaid's place seem almost inevitable, when she gets a letter from William at Bath, asking her to come over to England and join him at that gay and fashionable city. He would try to prepare her for singing at his concerts; but if after two years' trial she didn't succeed, he would take her back again to Hanover himself. In 1772, indeed, William in person came over to fetch her, and thenceforth the brother and sister worked unceasingly together in all their undertakings to the day of the great astronomer's death.

About this time Herschel had been reading Ferguson's "Astronomy," and felt very desirous of seeing for himself the objects in the heavens, invisible to the naked eye, of which he there found descriptions. For this purpose he must of course have a telescope. But how to obtain one? that was the question. There was a small two-and-a-half foot instrument on hire at one of the shops at Bath; and the ambitious organist borrowed this poor little glass for a time, not merely to look through, but to use as a model for constructing one on his own account. Buying was impossible, of course, for telescopes cost much money: but making would not be difficult for a determined mind. He had always been of a mechanical turn, and he was now fired with a desire to build himself a telescope eighteen or twenty feet long. He sent to London for the lenses, which could not be bought at Bath; and Carolina amused herself by making a pasteboard tube to fit them in her leisure hours. It was long before he reached twenty feet, indeed: his first effort was a seven-foot, attained only "after many continuous determined trials." The amateur pasteboard frame did not fully answer Herschel's expectations, so he was obliged to go in grudgingly for the expense of a tin tube. The reflecting mirror which he ought to have had proved too dear for his still slender purse, and he thus had to forego it with much regret. But he found a man at Bath who had once been in the mirror-polishing line; and he bought from him for a bargain all his rubbish of patterns, tools, unfinished mirrors and so forth, with which he proceeded to experiment on the manufacture of a proper telescope. In the summer, when the season was over, and all the great people had left Bath, the house, as Carolina says ruefully, "was turned into a workshop." William's younger brother Alexander was busy putting up a big lathe in a bedroom, grinding glasses and turning eyepieces; while in the drawing-room itself, sacred to William's aristocratic pupils, a carpenter, sad to relate, was engaged in making a tube and putting up stands for the future telescopes. Sad goings on, indeed, in the family of a respectable music-master and organist! Many a good solid shopkeeper in Bath must no doubt have shaken his grey head solemnly as he passed the door, and muttered to himself that that young German singer fellow was clearly going on the road to ruin with his foolish good-for-nothing star-gazing.

In 1774, when William Herschel was thirty six, he had at last constructed himself a seven-foot telescope, and began for the first time in his life to view the heavens in a systematic manner. From this he advanced to a ten-foot, and then to one of twenty, for he meant to see stars that no astronomer had ever yet dreamt of beholding. It was comparatively late in life to begin, but Herschel had laid a solid foundation already and he was enabled therefore to do an immense deal in the second half of those threescore years and ten which are the allotted average life of man, but which he himself really overstepped by fourteen winters. As he said long afterwards with his modest manner to the poet Campbell, "I have looked further into space than ever human being did before me. I have observed stars of which the light, it can be proved, must take two millions of years to reach this earth." That would have been a grand thing for any man to be able truthfully to say under any circumstances: it was a marvellous thing for a man who had laboured under all the original disadvantages of Herschel— a man who began life as a penniless German bandsman, and up to the age of thirty-six had never even looked through a telescope.

At this time, Herschel was engaged in playing the harpsichord in the orchestra of the theatre; and it was during the interval between the acts that he made his first general survey of the heavens. The moment his part was finished, he would rush out to gaze through his telescope; and in these short periods he managed to observe all the visible stars of what are called the first, second, third, and fourth magnitudes. Henceforth he went on building telescope after telescope, each one better than the last; and now all his glasses were ground and polished either by his own hand or by his brother Alexander's. Carolina meanwhile took her part in the workshop; but as she had also to sing at the oratorios, and her awkward German manners might shock the sensitive nerves of the Bath aristocrats, she took two lessons a week for a whole twelvemonth (she tells us in her delightfully straightforward fashion) "from Miss Fleming, the celebrated dancing mistress, to drill me for a gentlewoman." Poor Carolina, there she was mistaken: Miss Fleming could make her into no gentlewoman, for she was born one already, and nothing proves it more than the perfect absence of false shame with which in her memoirs she tells us all these graphic little details of their early humble days.

While they were thus working at Bath an incident occurred which is worth mentioning because it shows the very different directions in which the presence or the want of steady persistence may lead the various members of the very self-same family. William received a letter from his widowed mother at Hanover to say, in deep distress, that Dietrich, the youngest brother, had run away from home, it was supposed for the purpose of going to India, "with a young idler no older than himself." Forthwith, the budding astronomer left the lathe where he was busy turning an eye-piece from a cocoa-nut shell, and, like a good son and brother as he always was, hurried off to Holland and thence to Hanover. No Dietrich was anywhere to be found. But while he was away, Carolina at Bath received a letter from Dietrich himself, to tell her ruefully he was "laid up very ill" at a waterside tavern in Wapping—not the nicest or most savoury East End sailor-suburb of London. Alexander immediately took the coach to town, put the prodigal into a decent lodging, nursed him carefully for a fortnight, and then took him down with him in triumph to the family home at Bath. There brother William found him safe and sound on his return, under the sisterly care of good Carolina. A pretty dance he had led the two earnest and industrious astronomers; but they seem always to have treated this black sheep of the family with uniform kindness, and long afterwards Sir William remembered him favourably in his last will.

In 1779 and the succeeding years the three Herschels were engaged during all their spare time in measuring the heights of about one hundred mountains in the moon, which William gauged by three different methods. In the same year, he made an acquaintance of some importance to him, as forming his first introduction to the wider world of science in London and elsewhere. Dr. Watson, a Fellow of the Royal Society, happened, to see him working at his telescope; and this led to a visit from the electrician to the amateur astronomer. Dr. Watson was just then engaged in getting up a Philosophical Society at Bath (a far rarer institution at that time in a provincial town than now), and he invited William Herschel to join it. Here Herschel learned for the first time to mix with those who were more nearly his intellectual equals, and to measure his strength against other men's.

It was in 1781 that Herschel made the great discovery which immediately established his fame as an astronomer, and enabled him to turn from conducting concerts to the far higher work of professionally observing the stars. On the night of Tuesday, March 13th, Herschel was engaged in his usual systematic survey of the sky, a bit at a time, when his telescope lighted among a group of small fixed stars upon what he at first imagined to be a new comet. It proved to be no comet, however, but a true planet—a veritable world, revolving like our own in a nearly circular path around the sun as centre, though far more remote from it than the most distant planet then known, Saturn. Herschel called his new world the Georgium Sidus (King George's star) in honour of the reigning monarch; but it has since been known as Uranus. Astronomers all over Europe were soon apprised of this wonderful discovery, and the path of the freshly found planet was computed by calculation, its distance from the sun being settled at nineteen times that of our own earth.

In order faintly to understand the importance attached at the time to Herschel's observation of this very remote and seemingly petty world, we must remember that up to that date all the planets which circle round our own sun had been familiarly known to everybody from time immemorial. To suggest that there was yet another world belonging to our system outside the path of the furthest known planet would have seemed to most people like pure folly. Since then, we have grown quite accustomed to the discovery of a fresh small world or two every year, and we have even had another large planet (Neptune), still more remote than Herschel's Uranus, added to the list of known orbs in our own solar system. But in Herschel's day, nobody had ever heard of a new planet being discovered since the beginning of all things. A hundred years before, an Italian astronomer, it is true, had found out four small moons revolving round Saturn, besides the big moon then already known; but for a whole century, everybody believed that the solar system was now quite fully explored, and that nothing fresh could be discovered about it. Hence Herschel's observation produced a very different effect from, say, the discovery of the two moons which revolve round Mars, in our own day. Even people who felt no interest in astronomy were aroused to attention. Mr. Herschel's new planet became the talk of the town and the subject of much admiring discussion in the London newspapers. Strange, indeed, that an amateur astronomer of Bath, a mere German music-master, should have hit upon a planet which escaped the sight even of the king's own Astronomer Royal at Greenwich.

Of course there were not people wanting who ascribed this wonderful discovery of Herschel's to pure chance. If he hadn't just happened to turn his telescope in that particular direction on that particular night, he wouldn't have seen this Georgium Sidus they made such a fuss about at all. Quite so. And if he hadn't built a twenty-foot telescope for himself, he wouldn't have turned it anywhere at any time. But Herschel himself knew better. "This was by no means the result of chance," he said; "but a simple consequence of the position of the planet on that particular evening, since it occupied precisely that spot in the heavens which came in the order of the minute observations that I had previously mapped out for myself. Had I not seen it just when I did, I must inevitably have come upon it soon after, since my telescope was so perfect that I was able to distinguish it from a fixed star in the first minute of observation." Indeed, when once Herschel's twenty- foot telescope was made, he could not well have failed in the long run to discover Uranus, as his own description of his method clearly shows. "When I had carefully and thoroughly perfected the great instrument in all its parts," he says, "I made a systematic use of it in my observation of the heaven, first forming a determination never to pass by any, the smallest, portion of them without due investigation. This habit, persisted in, led to the discovery of the new planet (Georgium Sidus)." As well might one say that a skilled mining surveyor, digging for coal, came upon the seam by chance, as ascribe to chance the necessary result of such a careful and methodical scrutiny as this.

Before the year was out, the ingenious Mr. Herschel of Bath was elected a Fellow of the Royal Society, and was also presented with the Copley gold medal. From this moment all the distinguished people in Bath were anxious to be introduced to the philosophical music-master; and, indeed, they intruded so much upon his time that the daily music lessons were now often interrupted. He was soon, however, to give up lessons for ever, and devote himself to his more congenial and natural work in astronomy. In May, 1782, he went up to London, to be formally admitted to his Fellowship of the Royal Society. There he stayed so long that poor Carolina was quite frightened. It was "double the time which my brother could safely be absent from his scholars." The connection would be broken up, and the astronomy would be the ruin of the family. (A little of good old dame Herschel's housewifely leaven here, perhaps.) But William's letters from London to "Dear Lina" must soon have quieted her womanly fears. William had actually been presented to the king, and "met with a very gracious reception." He had explained the solar system to the king and queen, and his telescope was to be put up first at Greenwich and then at Richmond. The Greenwich authorities were delighted with his instrument; they have seen what Herschel calls "MY fine double stars" with it. "All my papers are printing," he tells Lina with pardonable pride, "and are allowed to be very valuable." But he himself is far from satisfied as yet with the results of his work. Evidently no small successes in the field of knowledge will do for William Herschel. "Among opticians and astronomers," he writes to Lina, "nothing now is talked of but WHAT THEY CALL my great discoveries. Alas! this shows how far they are behind, when such trifles as I have seen and done are called GREAT. Let me but get at it again! I will make such telescopes and see such things!" Well, well, William Herschel, in that last sentence we get the very keynote of true greatness and true genius.

But must he go back quietly to Bath and the toils of teaching? "An intolerable waste of time," he thought it. The king happily relieved him from this intolerable waste. He offered Herschel a salary of 200 pounds a year if he would come and live at Datchet, and devote himself entirely to astronomical observations. It was by no means a munificent sum for a king to offer for such labour; but Herschel gladly accepted it, as it would enable him to give up the interruption of teaching, and spend all his time on his beloved astronomy. His Bath friend, Sir William Watson, exclaimed when he heard of it, "Never bought monarch honour so cheap." Herschel was forty-three when he removed to Datchet, and from that day forth he lived almost entirely in his observatory, wholly given up to his astronomical pursuits. Even when he had to go to London to read his papers before the Royal Society, he chose a moonlight night (when the stars would be mostly invisible), so that it might not interfere with his regular labours.

Poor Carolina was horrified at the house at Datchet, which seemed terribly desolate and poor, even to her modest German ideas; but William declared his willingness to live permanently and cheerfully upon "eggs and bacon" now that he was at last free to do nothing on earth but observe the heavens. Night after night he and Carolina worked together at their silent task—he noting the small features with his big telescope, she "sweeping for comets" with a smaller glass or "finder." Herschel could have had no more useful or devoted assistant than his sister, who idolized him with all her heart. Alexander, too, came to stay with them during the slack months at Bath, and then the whole strength of the family was bent together on their labour of love in gauging the heavens.

But what use was it all? Why should they wish to go star-gazing? Well, if a man cannot see for himself what use it was, nobody else can put the answer into him, any more than they could put into him a love for nature, or for beauty, or for art, or for music, if he had it not to start with. What is the good of a great picture, a splendid oratorio, a grand poem? To the man who does not care for them, nothing; to the man who loves them, infinite. It is just the same with science. The use of knowledge to a mind like Herschel's is the mere possession of it. With such as he, it is a love, an object of desire, a thing to be sought after for its town sake; and the mere act of finding it is in itself purely delightful. "Happy is the man that findeth wisdom, and the man that getteth understanding. For the merchandise of it is better than the merchandise of silver, and the gain thereof than fine gold. She is more precious than rubies; and all the things thou canst desire are not to be compared unto her." So, to such a man as Herschel, that peaceful astronomer life at Datchet was indeed, in the truest sense of those much-abused words, "success in life." If you had asked some vulgar-minded neighbour of the great Sir William in his later days whether the astronomer had been a successful man or not, he would doubtless have answered, after his kind, "Certainly. He has been made a knight, has lands in two counties, and has saved 35,000 pounds." But if you had asked William Herschel himself, he would probably have said, with his usual mixture of earnestness and humility, "Yes, I have been a very fortunate man in life. I have discovered Uranus, and I have gauged all the depths of heaven, as none before ever gauged them, with my own great telescope."

Still, those who cannot sympathize with the pure love of knowledge for its own sake—one of the highest and noblest of human aims—should remember that astronomy is also of immense practical importance to mankind, and especially to navigation and commerce. Unless great astronomical calculations were correctly performed at Greenwich and elsewhere, it would be impossible for any ship or steamer to sail with safety from England to Australia or America. Every defect in our astronomical knowledge helps to wreck our vessels on doubtful coasts; every advance helps to save the lives of many sailors and the cargoes of many merchants. It is this practical utility of astronomy that justifies the spending of national money on observatories and transits of Venus, and it is the best apology for an astronomer's life to those who do not appreciate the use of knowledge for its own beauty.

At Datchet, Herschel not only made several large telescopes for sale, for which he obtained large prices, but he also got a grant of 2000 pounds from the king to aid him in constructing his huge forty-foot instrument. It was here, too, in 1783, that Herschel married. His wife was a widow lady of scientific tastes like his own, and she was possessed of considerable means, which enabled him henceforth to lay aside all anxiety on the score of money. They had but one child, a son, afterwards Sir John Herschel, almost as great an astronomer as his father had been before him. In 1785, the family moved to Clay Hall, in Old Windsor, and in 1786 to Slough, where Herschel lived for the remainder of his long life. How completely his whole soul was bound up in his work is shown in the curious fact recorded for us by Carolina Herschel. The last night at Clay Hall was spent in sweeping the sky with the great glass till daylight; and by the next evening the telescope stood ready for observations once more in the new home at Slough.

To follow Herschel through the remainder of his life would be merely to give a long catalogue of his endless observations and discoveries among the stars. Such a catalogue would be interesting only to astronomers; yet it would truly give the main facts of Herschel's existence in his happy home at Slough. Honoured by the world, dearly loved in his own family, and engrossed with a passionate affection for his chosen science, the great astronomer and philosopher grew grey in peace under his own roof, in the course of a singularly placid and gentle old age. In 1802 he laid before the Royal Society a list of five thousand new stars, star- clusters, or other heavenly bodies which he had discovered, and which formed the great body of his personal additions to astronomical knowledge. The University of Oxford made him Doctor of Laws, and very late in life he was knighted by the king—a too tardy acknowledgment of his immense services to science. To the very last, however, he worked on with a will; and, indeed, it is one of the great charms of scientific interest that it thus enables a man to keep his faculties on the alert to an advanced old age. In 1819, when Herschel was more than eighty, he writes to his sister a short note—"Lina, there is a great comet. I want you to assist me. Come to dine and spend the day here. If you can come soon after one o'clock, we shall have time to prepare maps and telescopes. I saw its situation last night. It has a long tail." How delightful to find such a living interest in life at the age of eighty!

On the 25th of August, 1822, this truly great and simple man passed away, in his eighty-fifth year. It has been possible here only to sketch out the chief personal points in his career, without dwelling much upon the scientific importance of his later life-long labours; but it must suffice to say briefly upon this point that Herschel's work was no mere mechanical star-finding; it was the most profoundly philosophical astronomical work ever performed, except perhaps Newton's and Laplace's. Among astronomers proper there has been none distinguished by such breadth of grasp, such wide conceptions, and such perfect clearness of view as the self- taught oboe-player of Hanover.

V.

JEAN FRANCOIS MILLET, PAINTER.

There is no part of France so singularly like England, both in the aspect of the country itself and in the features and character of the inhabitants, as Normandy. The wooded hills and dales, the frequent copses and apple orchards, the numerous thriving towns and villages, the towers and steeples half hidden among the trees, recall at every step the very similar scenery of our own beautiful and fruitful Devonshire. And as the land is, so are the people. Ages ago, about the same time that the Anglo-Saxon invaders first settled down in England, a band of similar English pirates, from the old common English home by the cranberry marshes of the Baltic, drove their long ships upon the long rocky peninsula of the Cotentin, which juts out, like a French Cornwall, from the mainland of Normandy up to the steep cliffs and beetling crags of busy Cherbourg. There they built themselves little hamlets and villages of true English type, whose very names to this day remind one of their ancient Saxon origin. Later on, the Danes or Northmen conquered the country, which they called after their own name, Normandy, that is to say, the Northmen's land. Mixing with the early Saxon or English settlers, and with the still more primitive Celtic inhabitants, the Northmen founded a race extremely like that which now inhabits our own country. To this day, the Norman peasants of the Cotentin retain many marks of their origin and their half-forgotten kinship with the English race. While other Frenchmen are generally dark and thick-set, the Norman is, as a rule, a tall, fair-haired, blue-eyed man, not unlike in build to our Yarmouth fisherman, or our Kentish labourers. In body and mind, there is something about him even now which makes him seem more nearly akin to us than the true Frenchmen who inhabit almost all the rest of France.

In the village of Gruchy, near Greville, in this wild and beautiful region of the Cotentin, there lived at the beginning of the present century a sturdy peasant family of the name of Millet. The father of the family was one of the petty village landholders so common in France; a labourer who owned and tilled his own tiny patch of farm, with the aid of his wife and children. We have now no class in England exactly answering to the French peasant proprietors, who form so large and important an element in the population just across the Channel. The small landholder in France belongs by position to about the same level as our own agricultural labourer, and in many ways is content with a style of dress and a mode of living against which English labourers would certainly protest with horror. And yet, he is a proprietor, with a proprietor's sense of the dignity of his position, and an ardent love of his own little much-subdivided corner of agricultural land. On this he spends all his energies, and however many children he may have, he will try to make a livelihood for all by their united labour out of the soil, rather than let one of them go to seek his fortune by any other means in the great cities. Thus the ground is often tilled up to an almost ridiculous extent, the entire labour of the family being sometimes expended in cultivating, manuring, weeding, and tending a patch of land perhaps hardly an acre in size. It is quite touching to see the care and solicitude with which these toilsome peasants will laboriously lay out their bit of garden with fruits or vegetables, making every line almost mathematically regular, planting every pea at a measured distance, or putting a smooth flat pebble under every strawberry on the evenly ridged-up vines. It is only in the very last resort that the peasant proprietor will consent to let one of his daughters go out to service, or send one of his sons adrift to seek his fortune as an artisan in the big, unknown, outer world.

Millet the elder, however, had nine children, which is an unusually large number for a French peasant family (where the women ordinarily marry late in life); and his little son Jean Francois (the second child and eldest boy), though set to weed and hoe upon the wee farm in his boyhood, was destined by his father for some other life than that of a tiller of the soil. He was born in the year before Waterloo—1814—and was brought up on his father's plot of land, in the hard rough way to which peasant children in France are always accustomed. Bronzed by sun and rain, poorly clad, and ill-fed, he acquired as a lad, from the open air and the toilsome life he led, a vigour of constitution which enabled him to bear up against the numerous hardships and struggles of his later days. "A Norman Peasant," he loved to call himself always, with a certain proud humility; and happily he had the rude health of one all his life long.

Hard as he worked, little Francois' time was not entirely taken up with attending to the fields or garden. He was a studious boy, and learned not only to read and write in French, but also to try some higher flights, rare indeed for a lad of his position. His family possessed remarkable qualities as French peasants go; and one of his great-uncles, a man of admirable strength of character, a priest in the days of the great Revolution, had braved the godless republicans of his time, and though deprived of his cure, and compelled to labour for his livelihood in the fields, had yet guided the plough in his priestly garments. His grandmother first taught him his letters; and when she had instructed him to the length of reading any French book that was put before him, the village priest took him in hand. In France, the priest comes often from the peasant class, and remains in social position a member of that class as long as he lives. But he always possesses a fair knowledge of Latin, the language in which all his religious services are conducted; and this knowledge serves as a key to much that his unlearned parishioners could never dream of knowing. Young Millet's parish priest taught him as much Latin as he knew himself; and so the boy was not only able to read the Bible in the Latin or Vulgate translation, but also to make acquaintance with the works of Virgil and several others of the great Roman poets. He read, too, the beautiful "Confessions" of St. Augustine, and the "Lives of the Saints," which he found in his father's scanty library, as well as the works of the great French preachers, Bossuet and Fenelon. Such early acquaintance with these and many other masterpieces of higher literature, we may be sure, helped greatly to mould the lad's mind into that grand and sober shape which it finally acquired.

Jean Francois' love of art was first aroused by the pictures in an old illustrated Bible which belonged to his father, and which he was permitted to look at on Sundays and festivals. The child admired these pictures immensely, and asked leave to be permitted to copy them. The only time he could find for the purpose, however, was that of the mid-day rest or siesta. It is the custom in France, as in Southern Europe generally, for labourers to cease from work for an hour or so in the middle of the day; and during this "tired man's holiday," young Millet, instead of resting, used to take out his pencil and paper, and try his hand at reproducing the pictures in the big Bible. His father was not without an undeveloped taste for art. "See," he would say, looking into some beautiful combe or glen on the hillside—"see that little cottage half buried in the trees; how beautiful it is! I think it ought to be drawn so—;" and then he would make a rough sketch of it on some scrap of paper. At times he would model things with a bit of clay, or cut the outline of a flower or an animal with his knife on a flat piece of wood. This unexercised talent Francois inherited in a still greater degree. As time went on, he progressed to making little drawings on his own account; and we may be sure the priest and all the good wives of Gruchy had quite settled in their own minds before long that Jean Francois Millet's hands would be able in time to paint quite a beautiful altar-piece for the village church.

By-and-by, when the time came for Francois to choose a trade, he being then a big lad of about nineteen, it was suggested to his father that young Millet might really make a regular painter—that is to say, an artist. In France, the general tastes of the people are far more artistic than with us; and the number of painters who find work for their brushes in Paris is something immensely greater than the number in our own smoky, money-making London. So there was nothing very remarkable, from a French point of view, in the idea of the young peasant turning for a livelihood to the profession of an artist. But Millet's father was a sober and austere man, a person of great dignity and solemnity, who decided to put his son's powers to the test in a very regular and critical fashion. He had often watched Francois drawing, and he thought well of the boy's work. If he had a real talent for painting, a painter he should be; if not, he must take to some other craft, where he would have the chance of making himself a decent livelihood. So he told Francois to prepare a couple of drawings, which he would submit to the judgment of M. Mouchel, a local painter at Cherbourg, the nearest large town, and capital of the department. Francois duly prepared the drawings, and Millet the elder went with his, son to submit them in proper form for M. Mouchel's opinion. Happily, M. Mouchel had judgment enough to see at a glance that the drawings possessed remarkable merit. "You must be playing me a trick," he said; "that lad could never have made these drawings." "I saw him do them with my own eyes," answered the father warmly. "Then," said Mouchel, "all I can say is this: he has in him the making of a great painter." He accepted Millet as his pupil; and the young man set off for Cherbourg accordingly, to study with care and diligence under his new master.

Cherbourg, though not yet at that time a great naval port, as it afterwards became, was a busy harbour and fishing town, where the young artist saw a great deal of a kind of life with which he possessed an immense sympathy. The hard work of the fishermen putting out to sea on stormy evenings, or toiling with their nets ashore after a sleepless night, made a living picture which stamped itself deeply on his receptive mind. A man of the people himself, born to toil and inured to it from babyhood, this constant scene of toiling and struggling humanity touched the deepest chord in his whole nature, so that some of the most beautiful and noble of his early pictures are really reminiscences of his first student days at

Cherbourg. But after he had spent a year in Mouchel's studio, sad news came to him from Gruchy. His father was dying, and Francois was only just in time to see him before he passed away. If the family was to be kept together at all, Francois must return from his easel and palette, and take once more to guiding the plough. With that earnest resolution which never forsook him, Millet decided to accept the inevitable. He went back home once more, and gave up his longings for art in order to till the ground for his fatherless sisters.

Luckily, however, his friends at Gruchy succeeded after awhile in sending him back again to Cherbourg, where he began to study under another master, Langlois, and to have hopes once more for his artistic future, now that he was free at last to pursue it in his own way. At this time, he read a great deal—Shakespeare, Walter Scott, Byron, Goethe's "Faust," Victor Hugo and Chateaubriand; in fact, all the great works he could lay his hands upon. Peasant as he was, he gave himself, half unconsciously, a noble education. Very soon, it became apparent that the Cherbourg masters could do nothing more for him, and that, if he really wished to perfect himself in art, he must go to Paris. In France, the national interest felt in painting is far greater and more general than in England. Nothing is commoner than for towns or departments to grant pensions (or as we should call them, scholarships) to promising lads who wish to study art in Paris. Young Millet had attracted so much attention at Cherbourg, that the Council General of the Department of the Manche voted him a present of six hundred francs (about 24 pounds) to start him on the way; and the town of Cherbourg promised him an annual grant of four hundred francs more (about 16 pounds). So up to Paris Millet went, and there was duly enrolled as a student at the Government "School of Fine-Arts."

Those student days in Paris were days of hunger and cold, very often, which Millet bore with the steady endurance of a Norman peasant boy. But they were also days of something worse to him—of effort misdirected, and of constant struggling against a system for which he was not fitted. In fact, Millet was an original genius, whereas the teachers at the School of Fine Arts were careful and methodical rule-of-thumb martinets. They wished to train Millet into the ordinary pattern, which he could not follow; and in the end, he left the school, and attached himself to the studio of Paul Delaroche, then the greatest painter of historical pictures in all Paris. But even Delaroche, though an artist of deep feeling and power, did not fully understand his young Norman pupil. He himself used to paint historical pictures in the grand style, full of richness and beauty; but his subjects were almost always chosen from the lives of kings or queens, and treated with corresponding calmness and dignity. "The Young Princes in the Tower," "The Execution of Marie Antoinette," "The Death of Queen Elizabeth," "Cromwell viewing the Body of Charles I."—these were the kind of pictures on which Delaroche loved to employ himself. Millet, on the other hand, though also full of dignity and pathos, together with an earnestness far surpassing Delaroche's, did not care for these lofty subjects. It was the dignity and pathos of labour that moved him most; the silent, weary, noble lives of the uncomplaining peasants, amongst whom his own days had been mostly passed. Delaroche could not make him out at all; he was such a curious, incomprehensible, odd young fellow! "There, go your own way, if you will," the great master said to him at last; "for my part, I can make nothing of you."

So, shortly after, Millet and his friend Marolle set up a studio for themselves in the Rue de l'Est in Paris. The precise occasion of their going was this. Millet was anxious to obtain the Grand Prize of Rome annually offered to the younger artists, and Delaroche definitely told him that his own influence would be used on behalf of another pupil. After this, the young Norman felt that he could do better by following out his own genius in his own fashion. At the Rue de l'Est, he continued to study hard, but he also devoted a large part of his time to painting cheap portraits— what artists call "pot-boilers;" mere hasty works dashed off anyhow to earn his daily livelihood. For these pictures he got about ten to fifteen francs apiece,—in English money from eight to twelve shillings. They were painted in a theatrical style, which Millet himself detested—all pink cheeks, and red lips, and blue satin, and lace collars; whereas his own natural style was one of great austerity and a certain earnest sombreness the exact reverse of the common Parisian taste to which he ministered. However, he had to please his patrons—and, like a sensible man, he went on producing these cheap daubs to any extent required, for a living, while he endeavoured to perfect himself meanwhile for the higher art he was meditating for the future. In the great galleries of the Louvre at Paris he found abundant models which he could study in the works of the old masters; and there, poring over Michael Angelo and Mantegna, he could recompense himself a little in his spare hours for the time he was obliged to waste on pinky-white faces and taffeta gowns. To an artist by nature there is nothing harder than working perforce against the bent of one's own innate and instinctive feelings.

In 1840, Millet found his life in Paris still so hard that he seemed for a time inclined to give up the attempt, and returned to Greville, where he painted a marine subject of the sort that was dearest to his heart— a group of sailors mending a sail. Shortly after, however, he was back in Paris—the record of these years of hard struggle is not very clear—with his wife, a Cherbourg girl whom he had imprudently married while still barely able to support himself in the utmost poverty. It was not till 1844 that the hard- working painter at last achieved his first success. It was with a picture of a milkwoman, one of his own favourite peasant subjects; and the poetry and sympathy which he had thrown into so commonplace a theme attracted the attention of many critics among the cultivated Parisian world of art. The "Milkwoman" was exhibited at the Salon (the great annual exhibition of works of art in Paris, like that of the Royal Academy in London, but on a far larger scale); and several good judges of art began immediately to inquire, "Who is Jean Francois Millet?" Hunting his address out, a party of friendly critics presented themselves at his lodgings, only to learn that Madame Millet had just died, and that her husband, half in despair, had gone back again once more to his native Norman hills and valleys.

But Millet was the last man on earth to sit down quietly with his hands folded, waiting for something or other to turn up. At Cherbourg, he set to work once more, no doubt painting more "pot- boilers" for the respectable shopkeepers of the neighbourhood— complacent portraits, perhaps, of a stout gentleman with a large watch-chain fully displayed, and of a stout lady in a black silk dress and with a vacant smile; and by hook or by crook he managed to scrape together a few hundred francs, with which once more he might return to Paris. But before he did so, he married again, this time more wisely. His wife, Catharine Lemaire, was a brave and good woman, who knew how to appreciate her husband, and to second him well in all his further struggles and endeavours. They went for a while to Havre, where Millet, in despair of getting better work, and not ashamed of doing anything honest to pay his way, actually took to painting sign-boards. In this way he saved money enough to make a fresh start in Paris. There, he continued his hard battle against the taste of the time; for French art was then dominated by the influence of men like Delaroche, or like Delacroix and Horace Vernet, who had accustomed the public to pictures of a very lofty, a very romantic, or a very fiery sort; and there were few indeed who cared for stern and sympathetic delineations of the French peasant's unlovely life of unremitting toil, such as Millet loved to set before them. Yet, in spite of discouragement, he did well to follow out this inner prompting of his own soul; for in that direction he could do his best work—and the best work is always the best worth doing in the long run. There are some minds, of which Franklin's is a good type, so versatile and so shifty that they can turn with advantage to any opening that chances to offer, no matter in what direction; and such minds do right in seizing every opportunity, wherever it occurs. But there are other minds, of which Gibson and Millet are excellent examples, naturally restricted to certain definite lines of thought or work; and such minds do right in persistently following up their own native talent, and refusing to be led aside by circumstances into any less natural or less promising channel.

While living in Paris at this time, Millet painted several of his favourite peasant pictures, amongst others "The Workman's Monday," which is a sort of parallel in painting to Burns's "Cotter's Saturday Night" in poetry. Indeed, there is a great deal in Millet which strongly reminds one at every step of Burns. Both were born of the agricultural labouring class; both remained peasants at heart, in feelings and sympathies, all their lives long; neither was ashamed of his origin, even in the days of his greatest fame; painter and poet alike loved best to choose their themes from the simple life of the poor whose trials and hardships they knew so well by bitter experience; and in each case they succeeded best in touching the hearts of others when they did not travel outside their own natural range of subjects. Only (if Scotchmen will allow one to say so) there was in Millet a far deeper vein of moral earnestness than in Burns; he was more profoundly impressed by the dignity and nobility of labour; in his tender sympathy there was a touch of solemn grandeur which was wanting in the too genial and easy-going Ayrshire ploughman.

In 1848, the year of revolutions, Millet painted his famous picture of "The Winnower," since considered as one of his finest works. Yet for a long time, though the critics praised it, it could not find a purchaser; till at last M. Ledru Rollin, a well-known politician, bought it for what Millet considered the capital price of five hundred francs (about 20 pounds). It would now fetch a simply fabulous price, if offered for sale. Soon after this comparative success Millet decided to leave Paris, where the surroundings indeed were little fitted to a man of his peculiarly rural and domestic tastes. He would go where he might see the living models of his peasant friends for ever before him; where he could watch them leaning over the plough pressed deep into the earth; cutting the faggots with stout arms in the thick-grown copses; driving the cattle home at milking time with weary feet, along the endless, straight white high-roads of the French rural districts. At the same time, he must be within easy reach of Paris; for though he had almost made up his mind not to exhibit any more at the Salon—people didn't care to see his reapers or his fishermen—he must still manage to keep himself within call of possible purchasers; and for this purpose he selected the little village of Barbizon, on the edge of the forest of Fontainebleau.

The woods of Fontainebleau stand to Paris in somewhat the same relation that Windsor Great Park stands to London; only, the scenery is more forest-like, and the trees are big and antique looking. By the outskirts of this great wood stands the pretty hamlet of Barbizon, a single long street of small peasant cottages, built with the usual French rural disregard of beauty or cleanliness. At the top of the street, in a little three-roomed house, the painter and his wife settled down quietly; and here they lived for twenty-seven years, long after Millet's name had grown to be famous in the history of contemporary French painting. An English critic, who visited the spot in the days of Millet's greatest celebrity, was astonished to find the painter, whom he had come to see, strolling about the village in rustic clothes, and even wearing the sabots or wooden shoes which are in France the social mark of the working classes, much as the smock-frock used once to be in the remoter country districts of England. Perhaps this was a little bit of affectation on Millet's part— a sort of proud declaration of the fact that in spite of fame and honours he still insisted upon counting himself a simple peasant; but if so, it was, after all, a very pretty and harmless affectation indeed. Better to see a man sticking pertinaciously to his wooden shoes, than turning his back upon old friends and old associations in the days of his worldly prosperity.

At Barbizon Millet's life moved on so quietly that there is nothing to record in it almost, save a long list of pictures painted, and a gradual growth, not in popularity (for THAT Millet never really attained at all), but in the esteem of the best judges, which of course brought with it at last, first ease, then comfort, and finally comparative riches. Millet was able now to paint such subjects as pleased him best, and he threw himself into his work with all the fervour of his intensely earnest and poetical nature. Whatever might be the subject which he undertook, he knew how to handle it so that it became instinct with his own fine feeling for the life he saw around him. In 1852 he painted his "Man spreading Manure." In itself, that is not a very exalted or beautiful occupation; but what Millet saw in it was the man, not the manure— the toiling, sorrowing, human fellow-being, whose labour and whose spirit he knew so well how to appreciate. And in this view of the subject he makes us all at once sympathize. Other pictures of this period are such as "The Gleaners," "The Reapers," "A Peasant grafting a Tree," "The Potato Planters," and so forth. These were very different subjects indeed from the dignified kings and queens painted by Delaroche, or the fiery battle-pieces of Delacroix but they touch a chord in our souls which those great painters fail to strike, and his treatment of them is always truthful, tender, melancholy, and exquisite.

Bit by bit, French artistic opinion began to recognize the real greatness of the retiring painter at Barbizon. He came to be looked upon as a true artist, and his pictures sold every year for increasingly large prices. Still, he had not been officially recognized; and in France, where everything, even to art and the theatre, is under governmental regulation, this want of official countenance is always severely felt. At last, in 1867, Millet was awarded the medal of the first class, and was appointed a Chevalier of the Legion of Honour. The latter distinction carries with it the right to wear that little tag of ribbon on the coat which all Frenchmen prize so highly; for to be "decorated," as it is called, is in France a spur to ambition of something the same sort as a knighthood or a peerage in England, though of course it lies within the reach of a far greater number of citizens. There is something to our ideas rather absurd in the notion of bestowing such a tag of ribbon on a man of Millet's aims and occupations; but all honours are honours just according to the estimation of the man who receives them and the society in which he lives; and Millet no doubt prized his admission to the Legion of Honour all the more because it had been so long delayed and so little truckled for.

To the end of his days, Millet never left his beloved Barbizon. He stopped there, wandering about the fields, watching peasants at work, imprinting their images firmly upon his eye and brain, and then going home again to put the figures he had thus observed upon his vivid canvas. For, strange to say, unlike almost every other great painter, Millet never painted from a model. Instead of getting a man or woman to sit for him in the pose he required, he would go out into the meadows and look at the men and women at their actual daily occupations; and so keen and acute was his power of observation, and so retentive was his inner eye, that he could then recall almost every detail of action or manner as clearly as if he had the original present in his studio before him. As a rule, such a practice is not to be recommended to any one who wishes to draw with even moderate accuracy; constant study of the actual object, and frequent comparison by glancing from object to copy, are absolutely necessary for forming a correct draughtsman. But Millet knew his own way best; and how wonderfully minute and painstaking must his survey have been when it enabled him to reproduce the picture of a person afterwards in every detail of dress or movement.

He did not paint very fast. He preferred doing good work to much work—an almost invariable trait of all the best workmen. During the thirty-one years that he worked independently, he produced only eighty pictures—not more, on an average, than two or three a year. Compared with the rate at which most successful artists cover canvas to sell, this was very slow. But then, Millet did not paint mainly to sell; he painted to satisfy his own strict ideas of what constituted the highest art. His pictures are usually very simple in their theme; take, for example, his "Angelus," painted at the height of his fame, in 1867. A man and a woman are working in the fields— two poor, simple-minded, weather-beaten, devout French peasants. It is nightfall; the bell called the "Angelus" rings out from the church steeple, and the two poor souls, resting for a moment from their labours, devote a few seconds to the silent prayers enjoined by their church. That is all; and yet in that one picture the sorrows, the toils, and the consolations of the needy French peasantry are summed up in a single glimpse of a pair of working and praying partners.

Millet died somewhat suddenly in 1875. Strong and hearty as he was, even the sturdy health of the Norman peasant had been undermined by the long hardships of his early struggles, and his constitution gave way at last with comparative rapidity. Still, he had lived long enough to see his fame established, to enjoy ten years of ease and honour, and to find his work cordially admired by all those for whose admiration he could have cared to make an effort. After his death, the pictures and unfinished sketches in his studio were sold for 321,000 francs, a little less than 13,000 pounds. The peasant boy of Greville had at last conquered all the difficulties which obstructed his path, and had fought his own way to fame and dignity. And in so fighting, he had steadily resisted the temptation to pander to the low and coarse taste in art of the men by whom he was surrounded. In spite of cold, and hunger, and poverty, he had gone on trying to put upon his canvas the purer, truer, and higher ideas with which his own beautiful soul was profoundly animated. In that endeavour he nobly succeeded. While too many contemporary French pictures are vicious and sensual in tone and feeling, every one of Millet's pictures is a sermon in colour—a thing to make us sympathize more deeply with our kind, and to send us away, saddened perhaps, yet ennobled and purified.

VI.

JAMES GARFIELD, CANAL BOY.

At the present time, the neighbourhood of Cleveland, Ohio, the busiest town along the southern shore of Lake Erie, may fairly rank as one of the richest agricultural districts in all America. But when Abram Garfield settled down in the township of Orange in 1830, it was one of the wildest and most unpeopled woodland regions in the whole of the United States. Pioneers from the older states had only just begun to make little clearings for themselves in the unbroken forest; and land was still so cheap that Abram Garfield was able to buy himself a tract of fifty acres for no more than 20 pounds. His brother-in-law's family removed there with him; and the whole strength of the two households was immediately employed in building a rough log hut for their common accommodation, where both the Garfields and the Boyntons lived together during the early days of their occupation. The hut consisted of a mere square box, made by piling logs on top of one another, the spaces between being filled with mud, while the roof was formed of loose stone slabs. Huts of that sort are everywhere common among the isolation of the American backwoods; and isolated indeed they were, for the Garfields' nearest neighbours, when they first set up house, lived as far as seven miles away, across the uncleared forest.

When Abram Garfield came to this lonely lodge in the primaeval woodlands, he had one son and one daughter. In 1831, the year after his removal to his new home, a second boy was born into the family, whom his father named James Abram. Before the baby was eighteen months old, the father died, and was buried alone, after the only possible fashion among such solitary settlers, in a corner of the wheat field which he himself had cleared of its stumps. A widow's life is always a hard one, but in such a country and under such conditions it is even harder and more lonely than elsewhere. Mrs. Garfield's eldest boy, Thomas, was only eleven years old; and with the aid of this one ineffectual helper, she managed herself to carry on the farm for many years. Only those who know the hard toil of a raw American township can have any idea what that really means. A farmer's work in America is not like a farmer's work in England. The man who occupies the soil is there at once his own landlord and his own labourer; and he has to contend with nature as nobody in England has had to contend with it for the last five centuries at least. He finds the land covered with trees, which he has first to fell and sell as timber; then he must dig or burn out the stumps; clear the plot of boulders and large stones; drain it, fence it, plough it, and harrow it; build barns for the produce and sheds for the cows; in short, MAKE his farm, instead of merely TAKING it. This is labour from which many strong men shrink in dismay, especially those who have come out fresh from a civilized and fully occupied land. For a woman and a boy, it is a task that seems almost above their utmost powers. Nevertheless, Mrs. Garfield and her son did not fail under it. With her own hands, the mother split up the young trees info rude triangular rails to make the rough snake fences of the country—mere zigzags of wood laid one bit above the other; while the lad worked away bravely at sowing fall and spring wheat, hoeing Indian corn, and building a little barn for the harvest before the arrival of the long cold Ohio winter. To such a family did the future President originally belong; and with them he must have shared those strong qualities of perseverance and industry which more than anything else at length secured his ultimate success in life.

For James Garfield's history differs greatly in one point from that of most other famous working men, whose stories have been told in this volume. There is no reason to believe that he was a man of exceptional or commanding intellect. On the contrary, his mental powers appear to have been of a very respectable but quite ordinary and commonplace order. It was not by brilliant genius that James Garfield made his way up in life; it was rather by hard work, unceasing energy, high principle, and generous enthusiasm for the cause of others. Some of the greatest geniuses among working men, such as Burns, Tannahill, and Chatterton, though they achieved fame, and though they have enriched the world with many touching and beautiful works, must be considered to have missed success in life, so far as their own happiness was concerned, by their unsteadiness, want of self-control, or lack of fixed principle. Garfield, on the other hand, was not a genius; but by his sterling good qualities he nevertheless achieved what cannot but be regarded as a true success, and left an honourable name behind him in the history of his country.

However poor an American township may be, it is seldom too poor to afford its children a moderate and humble education. While James Garfield was still very young, the settlers in the neighbourhood decided to import a schoolmaster, whom they "boarded about" between them, after a fashion very common in rural western districts. The school-house was only a log hut; the master was a lad of twenty; and the textbooks were of the very meagrest sort. But at least James Garfield was thus enabled to read and write, which after all is the great first step on the road to all possible promotion. The raw, uncouth Yankee lad who taught the Ohio boys, slept at Widow Garfield's, with Thomas and James; and the sons of the neighbouring settlers worked on the farm during the summer months, but took lessons when the long ice and snow of winter along the lake shore put a stop almost entirely for the time to their usual labours.

James continued at school till he was twelve years old, and then, his brother Thomas (being by that time twenty-one) went away by agreement still further west to Michigan, leaving young Jim to take his place upon the little farm. The fences were all completed, by this time; the barn was built, the ground was fairly brought under cultivation, and it required comparatively little labour to keep the land cropped after the rough fashion which amply satisfies American pioneers, with no rent to pay, and only their bare living to make out of the soil. Thomas was going to fell trees in Michigan, to clear land there for a farmer; and he proposed to use his earnings (when he got them) for the purpose of building a "frame house" (that is to say, a house built of planks) instead of the existing log hut. It must be added, in fairness, that hard as were the circumstances under which the young Garfields lived, they were yet lucky in their situation in a new country, where wages were high, and where the struggle for life is far less severe or competitive than in old settled lands like France and England. Thomas, in fact; would get boarded for nothing in Michigan, and so would be able easily to save almost all his high wages for the purpose of building the frame house.

So James had to take to the farm in summer, while in the winter he began to work as a sort of amateur carpenter in a small way. As yet he had lived entirely in the backwoods, and had never seen a town or even a village; but his education in practical work had begun from his very babyhood, and he was handy after the usual fashion of American or colonial boys—ready to turn his hand to anything that happened to present itself. In new countries, where everybody has not got neighbours and workmen within call, such rough-and-ready handiness is far more common than in old England. The one carpenter of the neighbourhood asked James to help him, on the proud day when Tom brought back his earnings from Michigan, and set about the building of the frame house, for which he had already collected the unhewn timber. From that first beginning, by the time he was thirteen, James was promoted to assist in building a barn;

and he might have taken permanently to a carpenter's life, had it not been that his boyish passion for reading had inspired him with an equal passion for going to sea. He had read Marryatt's novels and other sailor tales—what boy has not?—and he was fired with the usual childish desire to embark upon that wonderful life of chasing buccaneers, fighting pirates, capturing prizes, or hunting hidden treasure, which is a lad's brilliantly coloured fancy picture of an everyday sailor's wet, cold, cheerless occupation.

At last, when James was about fifteen, his longing for the sea grew so strong that his mother, by way of a compromise, allowed him to go and try his luck with the Lake Erie captains at Cleveland. Shipping on the great lakes, where one can see neither bank from the middle of the wide blue sheet of water, and where wrecks are unhappily as painfully frequent as on our own coasts, was quite sufficiently like going to sea to suit the adventurous young backwoodsman to the top of his bent. But when he got to Cleveland, a fortunate disappointment awaited him. The Cleveland captains declined his services in such vigorous seafaring language (not unmixed with many unnecessary oaths), that he was glad enough to give up the idea of sailoring, and take a place as driver of a canal boat from Cleveland to Pittsburg in Pennsylvania, the boat being under the charge of one of his own cousins. Copper ore was then largely mined on Lake Superior, where it is very abundant, carried by ship to Cleveland, down the chain of lakes, and there transferred to canal boats, which took it on to Pittsburg, the centre of a great coal and manufacturing district in Pennsylvania, to be smelted and employed in various local arts. Young Garfield stuck for a little while to the canal business. He plodded along wearily upon the bank, driving his still wearier horse before him, and carrying ore down to Pittsburg with such grace as he best might; but it didn't somehow quite come up to his fancy picture of the seaman's life. It was dull and monotonous, and he didn't care for it much. In genuine American language, "he didn't find it up to sample." The sea might be very well in its way; but a canal was a very different matter indeed. So after a fair trial, James finally gave the business up, and returned to his mother on the little homestead, ill and tired with his long tramping.

While he was at home, the schoolmaster of the place, who saw that the lad had abilities, was never tired of urging him to go to school, and do himself justice by getting himself a first-rate education, or at least as good a one as could be obtained in America. James was ready enough to take this advice, if the means were forthcoming; but how was he to do so? "Oh, that's easy enough," said young Bates, the master. "You'll only have to work out of hours as a carpenter, take odd jobs in your vacations, live plainly, and there you are." In England there are few schools where such a plan would be practicable; but in rough-and-ready America, where self-help is no disgrace, there are many, and they are all well attended. In the neighbouring town of Chester, a petty Baptist sect had started a young school which they named Geauga Seminary (there are no plain schools in America—they are all "academies" or "institutes"); and to this simple place young Garfield went, to learn and work as best he might for his own advancement. A very strange figure he must then have cut, indeed; for a person who saw him at the time described him as wearing a pair of trousers he had long outworn, rough cow-hide boots, a waistcoat much too short for him, and a thread-bare coat, with sleeves that only reached a little below the elbows. Of such stuff as that, with a stout heart and an eager brain, the budding presidents of the United States are sometimes made.

James soon found himself humble lodgings at an old woman's in Chester, and he also found himself a stray place at a carpenter's shop in the town, where he was able to do three hours' work out of school time every day, besides giving up the whole of his Saturday holiday to regular labour. It was hard work, this schooling and carpentering side by side; but James throve upon it; and at the end of the first term he was not only able to pay all his bill for board and lodging, but also to carry home a few dollars in his pocket by way of savings.

James stopped three years at the "seminary" at Chester; and in the holidays he employed himself by teaching in the little township schools among the country districts. There is generally an opening for young students to earn a little at such times by instructing younger boys than themselves in reading, writing, and arithmetic; and the surrounding farmers, who want schooling for their boys, are glad enough to take the master in on the "boarding round" system, for the sake of his usefulness in overlooking the lads in the preparation of their home lessons. It is a simple patriarchal life, very different from anything we know in England; and though Ohio was by this time a far more settled and populated place than when Abram Garfield first went there, it was still quite possible to manage in this extremely primitive and family fashion. The fact is, though luxuries were comparatively unknown, food was cheap and abundant; and a young teacher who was willing to put his heart into his work could easily earn more than enough to live upon in rough comfort. Sometimes the school-house was a mere log hut, like that in which young Garfield had been born; but, at any rate, it was work to do, and food to eat, and that alone was a great thing for a lad who meant to make his own way in the world by his own exertions.

Near the end of his third year at Chester, James met, quite accidentally, with a young man who had come from a little embryo "college," of the sort so common in rising American towns, at a place called Hiram in Ohio. American schools are almost as remarkable as American towns for the oddity and ugliness of their names; and this "college" was known by the queer and meaningless title of the "Eclectic Institute." It was conducted by an obscure sect who dub themselves "The Disciples' Church," to which young Garfield's father and mother had both belonged. His casual acquaintance urged upon him strongly the desirability of attending the institute; and James, who had already begun to learn Latin, and wished to learn more, was easily persuaded to try this particular school rather than any other.

In August, 1851, James Garfield, then aged nearly twenty, presented himself at the "Eclectic Institute," in the farm-labourer's clothes which were his only existing raiment. He asked to see the "president" of the school, and told him plainly that he wished to come there for education, but that he was poor, and if he came, he must work for his living. "What can you do?" asked the president. "Sweep the floors, light the fires, ring the bell, and make myself generally useful," answered the young backwoodsman. The president, pleased with his eagerness, promised to try him for a fortnight; and at the end of the fortnight, Garfield had earned his teaching so well that he was excused from all further fees during the remainder of his stay at the little institute. His post was by no mean an easy one, for he was servant-of-all-work as well as student; but he cared very little for that as long as he could gain the means for self-improvement.

Hiram was a small town, as ugly as its name. Twelve miles from a railway, a mere agricultural centre, of the rough back-country sort, all brand new and dreary looking, with a couple of wooden churches, half a dozen wooden shops, two new intersecting streets with wooden sidewalks, and that was all. The "institute" was a square brick block, planted incongruously in the middle of an Indian-corn plantation; and the students were the sons and daughters of the surrounding farmers, for (as in most western schools) both sexes were here educated together. But the place suited Garfield far better than an older and more dignified university would have done. The other students knew no more than he did, so that he did not feel himself at a disadvantage; they were dressed almost as plainly as himself; and during the time he was at Hiram he worked away with a will at Latin, Greek, and the higher mathematics, so as to qualify himself for a better place hereafter. Meanwhile, the local carpenter gave him plenty of planing to do, with which he managed to pay his way; and as he had to rise before five every morning to ring the first bell, he was under no danger of oversleeping himself. By 1853, he had made so much progress in his studies that he was admitted as a sort of pupil teacher, giving instruction himself in the English department and in rudimentary Greek and Latin, while he went on with his own studies with the aid of the other teachers.

James had now learnt as much as the little "Eclectic Institute" could possibly teach him, and he began to think of going to some better college in the older-settled and more cultivated eastern states, where he might get an education somewhat higher than was afforded him by the raw "seminaries" and "academies" of his native Ohio. True, his own sect, the "Disciples' Church," had got up a petty university of their own, "Bethany College" — such self-styled colleges swarm all over the United States; but James didn't much care for the idea of going to it. "I was brought up among the Disciples," he said; "I have mixed chiefly among them; I know little of other people; it will enlarge my views and give me more liberal feelings if a try a college elsewhere, conducted otherwise; if I see a little of the rest of the world." Moreover, those were stirring times in the States. The slavery question was beginning to come uppermost. The men of the free states in the north and west were beginning to say among themselves that they would no longer tolerate that terrible blot upon American freedom — the enslavement of four million negroes in the cotton-growing south. James Garfield felt all his soul stirred within him by this great national problem — the greatest that any modern nation has ever had to solve for itself. Now, his own sect, the Disciples, and their college, Bethany, were strongly tinctured with a leaning in favour of slavery, which young James Garfield utterly detested. So he made up his mind to having nothing to do with the accursed thing, but to go east to some New England college, where he would mix among men of culture, and where he would probably find more congenial feelings on the slavery question.

Before deciding, he wrote to three eastern colleges, amongst others to Yale, the only American university which by its buildings and surroundings can lay any claim to compare, even at a long distance, in beauty and associations, with the least among European universities. The three colleges gave him nearly similar answers; but one of them, in addition to the formal statement of terms and so forth, added the short kindly sentence, "If you come here, we shall be glad to do what we can for you." It was only a small polite phrase; but it took the heart of the rough western boy. If other things were about the same, he said, he would go to the college which offered him, as it were, a friendly grasp of the hand. He had saved a little money at Hiram; and he proposed now to go on working for his living, as he had hitherto done, side by side with his regular studies. But his brother, who was always kind and thoughtful to him, would not hear of this. Thomas had prospered meanwhile in his own small way, and he insisted upon lending James such a sum as would cover his necessary expenses for two years at an eastern university. James insured his life for the amount, so that Thomas might not be a loser by his brotherly generosity in case of his death before repayment could be made; and then, with the money safe in his pocket, he started off for his chosen goal, the Williams College, in one of the most beautiful and hilly parts of Massachusetts.

During the three years that Garfield was at this place, he studied hard and regularly, so much so that at one time his brain showed symptoms of giving way under the constant strain. In the vacations, he took a trip into Vermont, a romantic mountain state, where he opened a writing school at a little country village; and another into the New York State, where he engaged himself in a similar way at a small town on the banks of the lovely Hudson river. At college, in spite of his rough western dress and manners, he earned for himself the reputation of a thoroughly good fellow. Indeed, geniality and warmth of manner, qualities always much prized by the social American people, were very marked traits throughout of Garfield's character, and no doubt helped him greatly in after life in, rising to the high summit which he finally reached. It was here, too, that he first openly identified himself with the anti-slavery party, which was then engaged in fighting out the important question whether any new slave states should be admitted to the Union. Charles Sumner, the real grand central figure of that noble struggle, was at that moment thundering in Congress against the iniquitous extension of the slave-holding area, and was employing all his magnificent powers to assail the abominable Fugitive Slave Bill, for the return of runaway negroes, who escaped north, into the hands of their angry masters. The American colleges are always big debating societies, where questions of politics are regularly argued out among the students; and Garfield put himself at the head of the anti-slavery movement at his own little university. He spoke upon the subject frequently before the assembled students, and gained himself a considerable reputation, not only as a zealous advocate of the rights of the negro, but also as an eloquent orator and a powerful argumentative debater.

In 1856, Garfield took his degree at Williams College, and had now finished his formal education. By that time, he was a fair though not a great scholar, competently read in the Greek and Latin literatures, and with a good knowledge of French and German. He was now nearly twenty-five years old; and his experience was large and varied enough to make him already into a man of the world. He had been farmer, carpenter, canal driver, and student; he had seen the primitive life of the forest, and the more civilized society of the Atlantic shore; he had taught in schools in many states; he had supported himself for years by his own labours; and now, at an age when many young men are, as a rule, only just beginning life on their own account, he had practically raised himself from his own class into the class of educated and cultivated gentlemen. As soon as he had taken his degree, his old friends, the trustees of the "Eclectic Institute" at Hiram, proud of their former sweeper and bell-ringer, called him back at a good salary as teacher of Greek and Latin. It was then just ten years since he had toiled wearily along the tow-path of the Ohio and Pennsylvania Canal.

As a teacher, Garfield seems to have been eminently successful. His genial character and good-natured way of explaining things made him a favourite at once with the rough western lads he had to teach, who would perhaps have thought a more formal teacher stiff and stuckup. Garfield was one of themselves; he knew their ways and their manners; he could make allowances for their awkwardness and bluntness of speech; he could adopt towards them the exact tone which put them at home at once with their easy-going instructor. Certainly, he inspired all his pupils with an immense love and devotion for him; and it is less easy to inspire those feelings in a sturdy Ohio farmer than in most other varieties of the essentially affectionate human species.

From 1857 to 1861, Garfield remained at Hiram, teaching and working very hard. His salary, though a good one for the time and place, was still humble according to our English notions; but it sufficed for his needs; and as yet it would have seemed hardly credible that in only twenty years the Ohio schoolmaster would rise to be President of the United States. Indeed, it is only in America, that country of peculiarly unencumbered political action, where every kind of talent is most rapidly recognized and utilized, that this particular form of swift promotion is really possible. But while Garfield was still at his Institute, he was taking a vigorous part in local politics, especially on the slavery question. Whenever there was a political meeting at Hiram, the young schoolmaster was always called upon to take the anti-slavery side; and he delivered himself so effectively upon this favourite topic that he began to be looked upon as a rising political character. In America, politics are less confined to any one class than in Europe; and there would be nothing unusual in the selection of a schoolmaster who could talk to a seat in the local or general legislature. The practice of paying members makes it possible for comparatively poor men to offer themselves as candidates; and politics are thus a career, in the sense of a livelihood, far more than in any other country.

In 1858, Garfield married a lady who had been a fellow-student of his in earlier days, and to whom he had been long engaged. In the succeeding year, he got an invitation which greatly pleased and flattered him. The authorities at Williams College asked him to deliver the "Master's Oration" at their annual festival; an unusual compliment to pay to so young a man, and one who had so recently taken his degree. It was the first opportunity he had ever had for a pleasure-trip, and taking his young wife with him (proud indeed, we may be sure, at this earliest honour of his life, the precursor of so many more) he went to Massachusetts by a somewhat roundabout but very picturesque route, down the Great Lakes, through the Thousand Islands, over the St. Lawrence rapids, and on to Quebec, the only town in America which from its old-world look can lay claim to the sort of beauty which so many ancient European cities abundantly possess. He delivered his address with much applause, and returned to his Ohio home well satisfied with this pleasant outing.

Immediately on his return, the speech-making schoolmaster was met by a very sudden and unexpected request that he would allow himself to be nominated for the State legislature. Every state of the

Union has its own separate little legislative body, consisting of two houses; and it was to the upper of these, the Senate of Ohio, that James Garfield was asked to become a candidate. The schoolmaster consented; and as those were times of very great excitement, when the South was threatening to secede if a President hostile to the slave-owning interest was elected, the contest was fought out almost entirely along those particular lines. Garfield was returned as senator by a large majority, and took his seat in the Ohio Senate in January, 1860. There, his voice was always raised against slavery, and he was recognized at once as one of the ablest speakers in the whole legislature.

In 1861, the great storm burst over the States. In the preceding November, Abraham Lincoln had been elected President. Lincoln was himself, like Garfield, a self-made man, who had risen from the very same pioneer labourer class;—a wood-cutter and rail-splitter in the backwoods of Illinois, he had become a common boatman on the Mississippi, and had there improved his mind by reading eagerly in all his spare moments. With one of those rapid rises so commonly made by self-taught lads in America, he had pushed his way into the Illinois legislature by the time he was twenty-five, and qualified himself to practise as a barrister at Springfield. His shrewd original talents had raised him with wonderful quickness into the front ranks of his own party; and when the question between the North and South rose into the region of practical politics, Lincoln was selected by the republicans (the antislavery group) as their candidate for the Presidency of the United States. This selection was a very significant one in several ways; Lincoln was a very strong opponent of slavery, and his candidature showed the southern slave-owners that if the Republicans were successful in the contest, a vigorous move against the slave-holding oligarchy would at once be made. But it was also significant in the fact that Lincoln was a western man; it was a sign that the farmers and grangers of the agricultural west were beginning to wake up politically and throw themselves into the full current of American State affairs. On both these grounds, Lincoln's nomination must have been deeply interesting to Garfield, whose own life had been so closely similar, and who was destined, twenty years later, to follow him to the same goal.

Lincoln was duly elected, and the southern states began to secede. The firing upon Fort Sumter by the South Carolina secessionists was the first blow struck in that terrible war. Every man who was privileged to live in America at that time (like the present writer) cannot recall without a glow of recollection the memory of the wild eagerness with which the North answered that note of defiance, and went forth with overpowering faith and eagerness to fight the good fight on behalf of human freedom. Such a spontaneous outburst of the enthusiasm of humanity has never been known, before or since. President Lincoln immediately called for a supply of seventy-five thousand men. In the Ohio Senate, his message was read amid tumultuous applause; and the moment the sound of the cheers died away, Garfield, as natural spokesman of the republican party, sprang to his feet, and moved in a short and impassioned speech that the state of Ohio should contribute twenty thousand men and three million dollars as its share in the general preparations. The motion was immediately carried with the wildest demonstrations of fervour, and Ohio, with all the rest of the North, rose like one man to put down by the strong hand the hideous traffic in human flesh and blood.

During those fiery and feverish days, every citizen of the loyal states felt himself to be, in reserve at least, a possible soldier. It was necessary to raise, drill, and render effective in an incredibly short time a large army; and it would have been impossible to do so had it not been for the eager enthusiasm with which civilians of every sort enlisted, and threw themselves into their military duties with almost incredible devotion. Garfield felt that he must bear his own part in the struggle by fighting it out, not in the Senate but on the field; and his first move was to obtain a large quantity of arms from the arsenal in the doubtfully loyal state of Missouri. In this mission he was completely successful; and he was next employed to raise and organize two new regiments of Ohio infantry. Garfield, of course, knew absolutely nothing of military matters at that time; but it was not a moment to stand upon questions of precedence or experience; the born organizers came naturally to the front, and Garfield was one of them. Indeed, the faculty for organization seems innate in the American people, so that when it became necessary to raise and equip so large a body of men at a few weeks' notice, the task was undertaken offhand by lawyers, doctors, shopkeepers, and schoolmasters, without a minute's hesitation, and was performed on the whole with distinguished success.

When Garfield had organized his regiments, the Governor asked him to accept the post of colonel to one of them. But Garfield at first mistrusted his own powers in this direction. How should he, who had hitherto been poring chiefly over the odes of Horace (his favourite poet), now take so suddenly to leading a thousand men into actual battle? He would accept only a subordinate position, he said, if a regular officer of the United States army, trained at the great military academy at West Point, was placed in command. So the Governor told him to go among his own farmer friends in his native district, and recruit a third regiment, promising to find him a West Point man as colonel, if one was available. Garfield accepted the post of lieutenant-colonel, raised the 42nd Ohio regiment, chiefly among his own old pupils at Hiram, and set off for the seat of operations. At the last moment the Governor failed to find a regular officer to lead these raw recruits, every available man being already occupied, and Garfield found himself, against his will, compelled to undertake the responsible task of commanding the regiment. He accepted the task thus thrust upon him, and as if by magic transformed himself at once from a schoolmaster into an able soldier.

In less than one month, Colonel Garfield took his raw troops into action in the battle of Middle Creek, and drove the Confederate General Marshall, with far larger numbers, out of his intrenchments, compelling him to retreat into Virginia. This timely victory did much to secure the northern advance along the line of the Mississippi. During the whole of the succeeding campaign Garfield handled his regiment with such native skill and marked success that the Government appointed him Brigadier-General for his bravery and military talent. In spite of all his early disadvantages, he had been the youngest member of the Ohio Senate, and now he was the youngest general in the whole American army.

Shortly after, the important victory of Chickamauga was gained almost entirely by the energy and sagacity of General Garfield. For this service, he was raised one degree in dignity, receiving his commission as Major-General. He served altogether only two years and three months in the army.

But while Garfield was at the head of his victorious troops in Kentucky, his friends in Ohio were arranging, without his consent or knowledge, to call him away to a very different sphere of work. They nominated Garfield as their candidate for the United States House of Representatives at Washington. The General himself was unwilling to accede to their request, when it reached him. He thought he could serve the country better in the field than in Congress. Besides, he was still a comparatively poor man. His salary as Major-General was double that of a member of the House; and for his wife's and children's sake he hesitated to accept the lesser position. Had he continued in the army to the end of the war, he would doubtless have risen to the very highest honours of that stirring epoch. But President Lincoln was very anxious that Garfield should come into the Congress, where his presence would greatly strengthen the President's hands; and with a generous self- denial which well bespeaks his thorough loyalty, Garfield gave up his military post and accepted a place in the House of Representatives. He took his seat in December, 1863.

For seventeen years, General Garfield sat in the general legislature of the United States as one of the members for Ohio. During all that time, he distinguished himself most honourably as the fearless advocate of honest government, and the pronounced enemy of those underhand dodges and wire-pulling machinery which are too often the disgrace of American politics. He was opposed to all corruption and chicanery, especially to the bad system of rewarding political supporters with places under Government, which has long been the chief blot upon American republican institutions. As a person of stalwart honesty and singleness of purpose, he made himself respected by both sides alike. Politically speaking, different men will judge very differently of Garfield's acts in the House of Representatives. Englishmen especially cannot fail to remark that his attitude towards ourselves was almost always one of latent hostility; but it is impossible for anybody to deny that his conduct was uniformly guided by high principle, and a constant deference to what he regarded as the right course of action.

In 1880, when General Garfield had already risen to be the acknowledged leader of the House of Representatives, his Ohio supporters put him in nomination for the upper chamber, the Senate. They wished Garfield to come down to the state capital and canvas for support; but this the General would not hear of. "I never asked for any place yet," he said, "except the post of bell-ringer and general sweeper at the Hiram Institute, and I won't ask for one now." But at least, his friends urged, he would be on the spot to encourage and confer with his partisans. No, Garfield answered; if they wished to elect him they must elect him in his absence; he would avoid all appearance, even, of angling for office. The result was that all the other candidates withdrew, and Garfield was elected by acclamation.

After the election he went down to Ohio and delivered a speech to his constituents, a part of which strikingly illustrates the courage and independence of the backwoods schoolmaster. "During the twenty years that I have been in public life," he said, "almost eighteen of it in the Congress of the United States, I have tried to do one thing. Whether I was mistaken or otherwise, it has been the plan of my life to follow my conviction, at whatever personal cost to myself. I have represented for many years a district in Congress whose approbation I greatly desired; but though it may seem, perhaps, a little egotistical to say it, I yet desired still more the approbation of one person, and his name was Garfield. He is the only man that I am compelled to sleep with, and eat with, and live with, and die with; and if I could not have his approbation I should have bad companionship."

Only one higher honour could now fall to the lot of a citizen of the United States. The presidency was the single post to which Garfield's ambition could still aspire. That honour came upon him, like all the others, without his seeking; and it came, too, quite unexpectedly. Five months later, in the summer of 1880, the National Republican Convention met to select a candidate for their party at the forthcoming presidential election. Every four years, before the election, each party thus meets to decide upon the man to whom its votes will be given at the final choice. After one or two ineffectual attempts to secure unanimity in favour of other and more prominent politicians, the Convention with one accord chose James Garfield for its candidate—a nomination which was quite as great a surprise to Garfield himself as to all the rest of the world. He was elected President of the United States in November, 1880.

It was a marvellous rise for the poor canal boy, the struggling student, the obscure schoolmaster, thus to find himself placed at the head of one among the greatest nations of the earth. He was still less than fifty, and he might reasonably have looked forward to many years of a happy, useful, and honourable life. Nevertheless, it is impossible to feel that Garfield's death was other than a noble and enviable one. He was cut off suddenly in the very moment of his brightest success, before the cares and disappointments of office had begun to dim the pleasure of his first unexpected triumph. He died a martyr to a good and honest cause, and his death-bed was cheered and alleviated by the hushed sorrow and sympathy of an entire nation—one might almost truthfully add, of the whole civilized world.

From the first, President Garfield set his face sternly against the bad practice of rewarding political adherents by allowing them to nominate officials in the public service—a species of covert corruption sanctioned by long usage in the United States. This honest and independent conduct raised up for him at once a host of enemies among his own party. The talk which they indulged in against the President produced a deep effect upon a half-crazy and wildly egotistic French-Canadian of the name of Guiteau, who had emigrated to the States and become an American citizen. General Garfield had arranged a trip to New England in the summer of 1881, to attend the annual festival at his old school, the Williams College, Massachusetts; and for that purpose he left the White House (the President's official residence at Washington) on July 2. As he stood in the station of the Baltimore and Potomac Railway, arm in arm with Mr. Blaine, the Secretary of State, Guiteau approached him casually, and, drawing out a pistol, fired two shots in rapid succession, one of which took effect on the President above the third rib. The assassin was at once secured, and the wounded President was carried back carefully to the White House.

Almost everybody who reads this book will remember the long suspense, while the President lay stretched upon his bed for weeks and weeks together, with all Europe and America watching anxiously for any sign of recovery, and sympathizing deeply with the wounded statesman and his devoted wife. Every effort that was possible was made to save him, but the wound was past all surgical skill. After lingering long with the stored-up force of a good constitution, James Garfield passed away at last of blood-poisoning, more deeply regretted perhaps than any other man whom the present generation can remember.

It is only in America that precisely such a success as Garfield's is possible for people who spring, as he did, from the midst of the people. In old-settled and wealthy countries we must be content, at best, with slower and less lofty promotion. But the lesson of Garfield's life is not for America only, but for the whole world of workers everywhere. The same qualities which procured his success there will produce a different, but still a solid success, anywhere else. As Garfield himself fittingly put it, with his usual keen American common sense, "There is no more common thought among young people than the foolish one, that by-and-by something will turn up by which they will suddenly achieve fame or fortune. No, young gentlemen; things don't turn up in this world unless somebody turns them up."

VII.

THOMAS EDWARD, SHOEMAKER.

It is the object of this volume to set forth the lives of working men who through industry, perseverance, and high principle have raised themselves by their own exertions from humble beginnings. Raised themselves! Yes; but to what? Not merely, let us hope, to wealth and position, not merely to worldly respect and high office, but to some conspicuous field of real usefulness to their fellow men. Those whose lives we have hitherto examined did so raise themselves by their own strenuous energy and self-education. Either, like Garfield and Franklin, they served the State zealously in peace or war; or else, like Stephenson and Telford, they improved human life by their inventions and engineering works; or, again, like Herschel and Fraunhofer, they added to the wide field of scientific knowledge; or finally, like Millet and Gibson, they beautified the world with their noble and inspiring artistic productions. But in every one of these cases, the men whose lives we have been here considering did actually rise, sooner or later, from the class of labourers into some other class socially and monetarily superior to it. Though they did great good in other ways to others, they did still as a matter of fact succeed themselves in quitting the rank in which they were born, and rising to some other rank more or less completely above it.

Now, it will be clear to everybody that so long as our present social arrangements exist, it must be impossible for the vast mass of labouring men ever to do anything of the sort. It is to be desired, indeed, that every labouring man should by industry and thrift secure independence in the end for himself and his family; but however much that may be the case, it will still rest certain that the vast mass of men will necessarily remain workers to the last; and that no attempt to raise individual working men above their own class into the professional or mercantile classes can ever greatly benefit the working masses as a whole. What is most of all desirable is that the condition, the aims, and the tastes of working men, as working men, should be raised and bettered; that without necessarily going outside their own ranks, they should become more prudent, more thrifty, better educated, and wider- minded than many of their predecessors have been in the past. Under such circumstances, it is surely well to set before ourselves some examples of working men who, while still remaining members of their own class, have in the truest and best sense "raised themselves" so as to attain the respect and admiration of others whether their equals or superiors in the artificial scale. Dr. Smiles, who has done much to illustrate the history of the picked men among the labouring orders, has chosen two or three lives of such a sort for investigation, and from them we may select a single one as an example of a working man's career rendered conspicuous by qualities other than those that usually secure external success.

Thomas Edward, associate of the Linnean Society, though a Scotchman all his life long, was accidentally born (so to speak) at Gosport, near Portsmouth, on Christmas Day, 1814. His father was in the Fifeshire militia, and in those warlike days, when almost all the regulars were on the Continent, fighting Napoleon, militia regiments used to be ordered about the country from one place to another, to watch the coast or mount guard over the French prisoners, in the most unaccountable fashion. So it happened, oddly enough, that Thomas Edward, a Scotchman of the Scotch, was born close under the big forts of Portsmouth harbour.

After Waterloo, however, the Fifeshire regiment was sent home again; and the militia being before long disbanded, John Edward, our hero's father, went to live at Aberdeen, where he plied his poor trade of a hand-loom linen weaver for many years. It was on the green at Aberdeen, surrounded by small labourers' cottages, that Thomas Edward passed his early days. From his babyhood, almost, the boy had a strong love for all the beasties he saw everywhere around him; a fondness for birds and animals, and a habit of taming them which can seldom be acquired, but which seems with some people to come instinctively by nature. While Tam was still quite a child, he loved to wander by himself out into the country, along the green banks of the Dee, or among the tidal islands at the mouth of the river, overgrown by waving seaweeds, and fringed with great white bunches of blossoming scurvy-grass. He loved to hunt for crabs and sea-anemones beside the ebbing channels, or to watch the jelly-fish left high and dry upon the shore by the retreating water. Already, in his simple way, the little ragged bare-footed Scotch laddie was at heart a born naturalist.

Very soon, Tam was not content with looking at the "venomous beasts," as the neighbours called them, but he must needs begin to bring them home, and set up a small aquarium and zoological garden on his own account. All was fish that came to Tam's net: tadpoles, newts, and stickleback from the ponds, beetles from the dung-heaps, green crabs from the sea-shore—nay, even in time such larger prizes as hedgehogs, moles, and nestfuls of birds. Nothing delighted him so much as to be out in the fields, hunting for and taming these his natural pets.

Unfortunately, Tam's father and mother did not share the boy's passion for nature, and instead of encouraging him in pursuing his inborn taste, they scolded him and punished him bitterly for bringing home the nasty creatures. But nothing could win away Tam from the love of the beasties; and in the end, he had his own way, and lived all his life, as he himself afterwards beautifully put it, "a fool to nature." Too often, unhappily, fathers and mothers thus try to check the best impulses in their children, under mistaken notions of right, and especially is this the case in many instances as regards the love of nature. Children are constantly chidden for taking an interest in the beautiful works of creation, and so have their first intelligent inquiries and aspirations chilled at once; when a little care and sympathy would get rid of the unpleasantness of having white mice or lizards crawling about the house, without putting a stop to the young beginner's longing for more knowledge of the wonderful and beautiful world in whose midst he lives.

When Tam was nearly five years old, he was sent to school, chiefly no doubt to get him out of the way; but Scotch schools for the children of the working classes were in those days very rough hard places, where the taws or leather strap was still regarded as the chief instrument of education. Little Edward was not a child to be restrained by that particular form of discipline; and after he had had two or three serious tussles with his instructors, he was at last so cruelly beaten by one of his masters that he refused to return, and his parents, who were themselves by no means lacking in old Scotch severity, upheld him in his determination. He had picked up reading by this time, and now for a while he was left alone to hunt about to his heart's content among his favourite fields and meadows. But by the time he was six years old, he felt he ought to be going to work, brave little mortal that he was; and as his father and mother thought so too, the poor wee mite was sent to join his elder brother in working at a tobacco factory in the town, at the wages of fourteen-pence a week. So, for the next two years, little Tam waited upon a spinner (as the workers are called) and began life in earnest as a working man.

At the end of two years, however, the brothers heard that better wages were being given, a couple of miles away, at Grandholm, up the river Don. So off the lads tramped, one fast-day (a recognized Scotch institution), to ask the manager of the Grandholm factory if he could give them employment. They told nobody of their intention, but trudged away on their own account; and when they came back and told their parents what they had done, the father was not very well satisfied with the proposal, because he thought it too far for so small a boy as Tam to walk every day to and from his work. Tam, however, was very anxious to go, not only on account of the increased wages, but also (though this was a secret) because of the beautiful woods and crags round Grandholm, through which he hoped to wander during the short dinner hour. In the end, John Edward gave way, and the boys were allowed to follow their own fancy in going to the new factory.

It was very hard work; the hours were from six in the morning till eight at night, for there was no Factory Act then to guard the interest of helpless children; so the boys had to be up at four in the morning, and were seldom home again till nine at night. In winter, the snow lies long and deep on those chilly Aberdeenshire roads, and the east winds from the German Ocean blow cold and cutting up the narrow valley of the Don; and it was dreary work toiling along them in the dark of morning or of night in bleak and cheerless December weather. Still, Tam liked it on the whole extremely well. His wages were now three shillings a week; and then, twice a day in summer, there was the beautiful walk to and fro along the leafy high-road. "People may say of factories what they please," Edward wrote much later, "but I liked this factory. It was a happy time for me whilst I remained there. The woods were easy of access during our meal-hours. What lots of nests! What insects, wild flowers, and plants, the like of which I had never seen before." The boy revelled in the beauty of the birds and beasts he saw here, and he retained a delightful recollection of them throughout his whole after life.

This happy time, however, was not to last for ever. When young Edward was eleven years old, his father took him away from Grandholm, and apprenticed him to a working shoemaker. The apprenticeship was to go on for six years; the wages to begin at eighteen-pence a week; and the hours, too sadly long, to be from six in the morning till nine at night. Tam's master, one Charles Begg, was a drunken London workman, who had wandered gradually north; a good shoemaker, but a quarrelsome, rowdy fellow, loving nothing on earth so much as a round with his fists on the slightest provocation. From this unpromising teacher, Edward took his first lessons in the useful art of shoemaking; and though he learned fast— for he was not slothful in business—he would have learned faster, no doubt, but for his employer's very drunken and careless ways. When Begg came home from the public-house, much the worse for whisky, he would first beat Tam, and then proceed upstairs to beat his wife. For three years young Edward lived under this intolerable tyranny, till he could stand it no longer. At last, Begg beat and ill-treated him so terribly that Tam refused outright to complete his apprenticeship. Begg was afraid to compel him to do so—doubtless fearing to expose his ill-usage of the lad. So Tam went to a new master, a kindly man, with whom he worked in future far more happily.

The boy now began to make himself a little botanical garden in the back yard of his mother's house—a piece of waste ground covered with rubbish, such as one often sees behind the poorer class of cottages in towns. Tam determined to alter all that, so he piled up all the stones into a small rockery, dug up the plot, manured it, and filled it with wild and garden flowers. The wild flowers, of course, he found in the woods and hedgerows around him; but the cultivated kinds he got in a very ingenious fashion, by visiting all the rubbish heaps of the neighbourhood, on which garden refuse was usually piled. A good many roots and plants can generally be found in such places, and by digging them up, Tam was soon able to make himself a number of bright and lively beds. Such self-help in natural history always lay very much in Edward's way.

At the same time, young Edward was now beginning to feel the desire for knowing something more about the beasts and birds of which he was so fond. He used to go in all his spare moments among the shops in the town, to look at the pictures in the windows, especially the pictures of animals; and though his earnings were still small, he bought a book whenever he was able to afford one. In those days, cheap papers for the people were only just beginning to come into existence; and Tam, who was now eighteen, bought the first number of the Penny Magazine, an excellent journal of that time, which he liked so much that he continued to take in the succeeding numbers. Some of the papers in it were about natural history, and these, of course, particularly delighted the young man's heart. He also bought the Weekly Visitor, which he read through over and over again.

In 1831, when Tam was still eighteen, he enlisted in the Aberdeenshire militia, and during his brief period of service an amusing circumstance occurred which well displays the almost irresistible character of Edward's love of nature. While he was drilling with the awkward squad one morning, a butterfly of a kind that he had never seen before happened to flit in front of him as he stood in the ranks. It was a beautiful large brown butterfly, and Edward was so fascinated by its appearance that he entirely forgot, in a moment, where he was and what he was doing. Without a second's thought, he darted wildly out of the ranks, and rushed after the butterfly, cap in hand. It led him a pretty chase, over sandhills and shore, for five minutes. He was just on the point of catching it at last, when he suddenly felt a heavy hand laid upon his shoulder, and looking round, he saw the corporal of the company and several soldiers come to arrest him. Such a serious offence against military discipline might have cost him dear indeed, for corporals have little sympathy with butterfly hunting; but luckily for Edward, as he was crossing the parade ground under arrest, he happened to meet an officer walking with some ladies. The officer asked the nature of his offence, and when the ladies heard what it was they were so much interested in such a strange creature as a butterfly-loving militiaman, that they interceded for him, and finally begged him off his expected punishment. The story shows us what sort of stuff Edward was really made of. He felt so deep an interest in all the beautiful living creatures around him for their own sake, that he could hardly restrain his feelings even under the most untoward circumstances.

When Edward was twenty, he removed from Aberdeen to Banff where he worked as a journeyman for a new master. The hours were very long, but by taking advantage of the summer evenings, he was still able to hunt for his beloved birds, caterpillars, and butterflies. Still, the low wages in the trade discouraged him much, and he almost made up his mind to save money and emigrate to America. But one small accident alone prevented him from carrying out this purpose. Like a good many other young men, the naturalist shoemaker fell in love. Not only so, but his falling in love took practical shape a little later in his getting married; and at twenty-three, the lonely butterfly hunter brought back a suitable young wife to his little home. The marriage was a very happy one. Mrs. Edward not only loved her husband deeply, but showed him sympathy in his favourite pursuits, and knew how to appreciate his sterling worth. Long afterwards she said, that though many of her neighbours could not understand her husband's strange behaviour, she had always felt how much better it was to have one who spent his spare time on the study of nature than one who spent it on the public-house.

As soon as Edward got a home of his own, he began to make a regular collection of all the animals and plants in Banffshire. This was a difficult thing for him to do, for he knew little of books, and had access to very few, so that he couldn't even find out the names of all the creatures he caught and preserved. But, though he didn't always know what they were called, he did know their natures and habits and all about them; and such first-hand knowledge in natural history is really the rarest and the most valuable of all. He saw little of his fellow-workmen. They were usually a drunken, careless lot; Edward was sober and thoughtful, and had other things to think of than those that they cared to talk about with one another. But he went out much into the fields, with invincible determination, having made up his mind that he would get to know all about the plants and beasties, however much the knowledge might cost him.

For this object, he bought a rusty old gun for four-and-sixpence, and invested in a few boxes and bottles for catching insects. His working hours were from six in the morning till nine at night, and for that long day he always worked hard to support his wife, and (when they came) his children. He had therefore only the night hours between nine and six to do all his collecting. Any other man, almost, would have given up the attempt as hopeless; but Edward resolved never to waste a single moment or a single penny, and by care and indomitable energy he succeeded in making his wished-for collection. Sometimes he was out tramping the whole night; sometimes he slept anyhow, under a hedge or haystack; sometimes he took up temporary quarters in a barn, an outhouse, or a ruined castle. But night after night he went on collecting, whenever he was able; and he watched the habits and manners of the fox, the badger, the otter, the weasel, the stoat, the pole-cat, and many other regular night-roamers as no one else, in all probability, had ever before watched them in the whole world.

Sometimes he suffered terrible disappointments, due directly or indirectly to his great poverty. Once, he took all his cases of insects, containing nine hundred and sixteen specimens, and representing the work of four years, up to his garret to keep them there till he was able to glaze them. When he came to take them down again he found to his horror that rats had got at the boxes, eaten almost every insect in the whole collection, and left nothing behind but the bare pins, with a few scattered legs, wings, and bodies, sticking amongst them. Most men would have been so disgusted with this miserable end to so much labour, that they would have given up moth hunting for ever. But Edward was made of different stuff. He went to work again as zealously as ever, and in four years more, he had got most of the beetles, flies, and chafers as carefully collected as before.

By the year 1845, Edward had gathered together about two thousand specimens of beasts, birds, and insects found in the neighbourhood of his own town of Banff. He made the cases to hold them himself, and did it so neatly that, in the case of his shells, each kind had even a separate little compartment all of its own. And now he unfortunately began to think of making money by exhibiting his small museum. If only he could get a few pounds to help him in buying books, materials, perhaps even a microscope, to help him in prosecuting his scientific work, what a magnificent thing that would be for him! Filled with this grand idea, he took a room in the Trades Hall at Banff, and exhibited his collection during a local fair. A good many people came to see it, and the Banff paper congratulated the poor shoemaker on his energy in gathering together such a museum of curiosities "without aid, and under discouraging circumstances which few would have successfully encountered." He was so far lucky in this first venture that he covered his expenses and was able even to put away a little money for future needs. Encouraged by this small triumph, the unwearied naturalist set to work during the next year, and added several new attractions to his little show. At the succeeding fair he again exhibited, and made still more money out of his speculation. Unhappily, the petty success thus secured led him to hope he might do even better by moving his collection to Aberdeen.

To Aberdeen, accordingly, Edward went. He took a shop in the great gay thoroughfare of that cold northern city—Union Street—and prepared to receive the world at large, and to get the money for the longed-for books and the much-desired microscope. Now, Aberdeen is a big, busy, bustling town; it has plenty of amusements and recreations; it has two colleges and many learned men of its own; and the people did not care to come and see the working shoemaker's poor small collection. If he had been a president of the British Association for the Advancement of Science, now—some learned knight or baronet come down by special train from London— the Aberdeen doctors and professors might have rushed to hear his address; or if he had been a famous music-hall singer or an imitation negro minstrel, the public at large might have flocked to be amused and degraded by his parrot-like buffoonery; but as he was only a working shoemaker from Banff, with a heaven-born instinct for watching and discovering all the strange beasts and birds of Scotland, and the ways and thoughts of them, why, of course, respectable Aberdeen, high or low, would have nothing in particular to say to him. Day after day went by, and hardly anybody came, till at last poor Edward's heart sank terribly within him. Even the few who did come were loth to believe that a working shoemaker could ever have gathered together such a large collection by his own exertions.

"Do you mean to say," said one of the Aberdeen physicians to Edward, "that you've maintained your wife and family by working at your trade, all the while that you've been making this collection?"

"Yes, I do," Edward answered.

"Oh, nonsense!" the doctor said. "How is it possible you could have done that?"

"By never losing a single minute or part of a minute," was the brave reply, "that I could by any means improve."

It is wonderful indeed that when once Edward had begun to attract anybody's attention at all, he and his exhibition should ever have been allowed to pass so unnoticed in a great, rich, learned city like Aberdeen. But it only shows how very hard it is for unassuming merit to push its way; for the Aberdeen people still went unheeding past the shop in Union Street, till Edward at last began to fear and tremble as to how he should ever meet the expenses of the exhibition. After the show had been open four weeks, one black Friday came when Edward never took a penny the whole day. As he sat there alone and despondent in the empty room, the postman brought him a letter. It was from his master at Banff. "Return immediately," it said, "or you will be discharged." What on earth could he do? He couldn't remove his collection; he couldn't pay his debt. A few more days passed, and he saw no way out of it. At last, in blank despair, he offered the whole collection for sale. A gentleman proposed to pay him the paltry sum of 20 pounds 10s. for the entire lot, the slow accumulations of ten long years. It was a miserable and totally inadequate price, but Edward could get no more. In the depths of his misery, he accepted it. The gentleman took the collection home, gave it to his boy, and finally allowed it all, for want of care and attention, to go to rack and ruin. And so that was the end of ten years of poor Thomas Edward's unremitting original work in natural history. A sadder tale of unrequited labour in the cause of science has seldom been written.

How he ever recovered from such a downfall to all his hopes and expectations is extraordinary. But the man had a wonderful power of bearing up against adverse circumstances; and when, after six weeks' absence, he returned to Banff, ruined and dispirited, he set to work once more, as best he might, at the old, old trade of shoemaking. He was obliged to leave his wife and children in Aberdeen, and to tramp himself on foot to Banff, so that he might earn the necessary money to bring them back; for the cash he had got for the collection had all gone in paying expenses. It is almost too sad to relate; and no wonder poor Edward felt crushed indeed when he got back once more to his lonely shoemaker's bench and fireless fireside. He was very lonely until his wife and children came. But when the carrier generously brought them back free (with that kindliness which the poor so often show to the poor), and the home was occupied once more, and the fire lighted, he felt as if life might still be worth living, at least for his wife and children. So he went back to his trade as heartily as he might, and worked at it well and successfully. For it is to be noted, that though Thomas Edward was so assiduous a naturalist and collector, he was the best hand, too, at making first-class shoes in all Banff. The good workman is generally the best man at whatever he undertakes. Certainly the best man is almost always a good workman at his own trade.

But of course he made no more natural history collections? Not a bit of it. Once a naturalist, always a naturalist. Edward set to work once more, nothing daunted, and by next spring he was out everywhere with his gun, exactly as before, replacing the sold collection as fast as ever his hand was able.

By this time Edward began to make a few good friends. Several magistrates for the county signed a paper for him, stating that they knew him to be a naturalist, and no poacher; and on presenting this paper to the gamekeepers, he was generally allowed to pursue his researches wherever he liked, and shoot any birds or animals he needed for his new museum. Soon after his return from Aberdeen, too, he made the acquaintance of a neighbouring Scotch minister, Mr. Smith of Monquhitter, who proved a very kind and useful friend to him. Mr. Smith was a brother naturalist, and he had books— those precious books—which he lent Edward freely; and there for the first time the shoemaker zoologist learned the scientific names of many among the birds and animals with whose lives and habits he had been so long familiar. Another thing the good minister did for his shoemaker friend: he constantly begged him to write to scientific journals the results of his observations in natural history. At first Edward was very timid; he didn't like to appear in print; thought his grammar and style wouldn't be good enough; fought shy of the proposal altogether. But at last Edward made up his mind to contribute a few notes to the Banffshire Journal, and from that he went on slowly to other papers, until at last he came to be one of the most valued occasional writers for several of the leading scientific periodicals in England. Unfortunately, science doesn't pay. All this work was done for love only; and Edward's only reward was the pleasure he himself derived from thus jotting down the facts he had observed about the beautiful creatures he loved so well.

Soon Mr. Smith induced the indefatigable shoemaker to send a few papers on the birds and beasts to the Zoologist. Readers began to perceive that these contributions were sent by a man of the right sort—a man who didn't merely read what other men had said about the creatures in books, but who watched their ways on his own account, and knew all about their habits and manners in their own homes. Other friends now began to interest themselves in him; and Edward obtained at last, what to a man of his tastes must have been almost as much as money or position—the society of people who could appreciate him, and could sympathize in all that interested him. Mr. Smith in particular always treated him, says Dr. Smiles, "as one intelligent man treats another." The paltry distinctions of artificial rank were all forgotten between them, and the two naturalists talked together with endless interest about all those lovely creatures that surround us every one on every side, but that so very few people comparatively have ever eyes to see or hearts to understand. It was a very great loss to Edward when Mr. Smith died, in 1854.

In the year 1858 the untiring shoemaker had gathered his third and last collection, the finest and best of all. By this time he had become an expert stuffer of birds, and a good preserver of fish and flowers. But his health was now beginning to fail. He was forty- four, and he had used his constitution very severely, going out at nights in cold and wet, and cheating himself of sleep during the natural hours of rest and recuperation. Happily, during all these years, he had resisted the advice of his Scotch labouring friends, to take out whisky with him on his nightly excursions. He never took a drop of it, at home or abroad. If he had done so, he himself believed, he could not have stood the cold, the damp, and the exposure in the way he did. His food was chiefly oatmeal-cake; his drink was water. "Sometimes, when I could afford it," he says, "my wife boiled an egg or two, and these were my only luxuries." He had a large family, and the task of providing for them was quite enough for his slender means, without leaving much margin for beer or whisky.

But the best constitution won't stand privation and exposure for ever. By-and-by Edward fell ill, and had a fever. He was ill for a month, and when he came round again the doctor told him that he must at once give up his nightly wandering. This was a real and serious blow to poor Edward; it was asking him to give up his one real pleasure and interest in life. All the happiest moments he had ever known were those which he had spent in the woods and fields, or among the lonely mountains with the falcons, and the herons, and the pine-martens, and the ermines. All this delightful life he was now told he must abandon for ever. Nor was that all. Illness costs money. While a man is earning nothing, he is running up a doctor's bill. Edward now saw that he must at last fall back upon his savings bank, as he rightly called it—his loved and cherished collection of Banffshire animals. He had to draw upon it heavily. Forty cases of birds were sold; and Edward now knew that he would never be able to replace the specimens he had parted with.

Still, his endless patience wasn't yet exhausted. No more of wandering by night, to be sure, upon moor or fell, gun in hand, chasing the merlin or the polecat to its hidden lair; no more of long watching after the snowy owl or the long-tailed titmouse among the frozen winter woods; but there remained one almost untried field on which Edward could expend his remaining energy, and in which he was to do better work for science than in all the rest— the sea.

This new field he began to cultivate in a novel and ingenious way. He got together all the old broken pails, pots, pans, and kettles he could find in the neighbourhood, filled them with straw or bits of rag, and then sank them with a heavy stone into the rocky pools that abound along that weather-beaten coast. A rope was tied to one end, by which he could raise them again; and once a month he used to go his rounds to visit these very primitive but effectual sea-traps. Lots of living things had meanwhile congregated in the safe nests thus provided for them, and Edward sorted them all over, taking home with him all the newer or more valuable specimens. In this way he was enabled to make several additions to our knowledge of the living things that inhabit the sea off the north-east coast of Scotland.

The fishermen also helped him not a little, by giving him many rare kinds of fish or refuse from their nets, which he duly examined and classified. As a rule, the hardy men who go on the smacks have a profound contempt for natural history, and will not be tempted, even by offers of money, to assist those whom they consider as half-daft gentlefolk in what seems to them a perfectly useless and almost childish amusement. But it was different with Tam Edward, the strange shoemaker whom they all knew so well; if HE wanted fish or rubbish for his neat collection in the home-made glass cases, why, of course he could have them, and welcome. So they brought him rare sand-suckers, and blue-striped wrasse, and saury pike, and gigantic cuttle-fish, four feet long, to his heart's content. Edward's daughters were now also old enough to help him in his scientific studies. They used to watch for the clearing of the nets, and pick out of the refuse whatever they thought would interest or please their father. But the fish themselves were Edward's greatest helpers and assistants. As Dr. Smiles quaintly puts it, they were the best of all possible dredgers. His daughters used to secure him as many stomachs as possible, and from their contents he picked out an immense number of beautiful and valuable specimens. The bill of fare of the cod alone comprised an incredible variety of small crabs, shells, shrimps, sea-mice, star- fish, jelly-fish, sea anemones, eggs, and zoophytes. All these went to swell Edward's new collection of marine animals.

To identify and name so many small and little-known creatures was a very difficult task for the poor shoemaker, with so few books, and no opportunities for visiting museums and learned societies. But his industry and ingenuity managed to surmount all obstacles. Naturalists everywhere are very willing to aid and instruct one another; especially are the highest authorities almost always eager to give every help and encouragement in their power to local amateurs. Edward used to wait till he had collected a batch of specimens of a single class or order, and then he would send them by post to learned men in different parts of the country, who named them for him, and sent them back with some information as to their proper place in the classification of the group to which they belonged. Mr. Spence Bate of Plymouth is the greatest living authority on crustaceans, such as the lobsters, shrimps, sea-fleas, and hermit crabs; and to him Edward sent all the queer crawling things of that description that he found in his original sea-traps. Mr. Couch, of Polperro in Cornwall, was equally versed in the true backboned fishes; and to him Edward sent any doubtful midges, or gurnards, or gobies, or whiffs. So numerous are the animals and plants of the sea-shore, even in the north of Scotland alone, that if one were to make a complete list of all Edward's finds it would occupy an entire book almost as large as this volume.

Naturalists now began to help Edward in another way, the way that he most needed, by kind presents of books, especially their own writings—a kind of gift which cost them nothing, but was worth to him a very great deal. Mr. Newman, the editor of the Zoologist paper, was one of his most useful correspondents, and gave him several excellent books on natural history. Mr. Bate made him a still more coveted present—a microscope, with which he could examine several minute animals, too small to be looked at by the naked eye. The same good friend also gave him a little pocket-lens (or magnifying glass) for use on the sea-shore.

As Edward went on, his knowledge increased rapidly, and his discoveries fully kept pace with it. The wretchedly paid Banff shoemaker was now corresponding familiarly with half the most eminent men of science in the kingdom, and was a valued contributor to all the most important scientific journals. Several new animals which he had discovered were named in his honour, and frequent references were made to him in printed works of the first importance. It occurred to Mr. Couch and Mr. Bate, therefore, both of whom were greatly indebted to the working-man naturalist for specimens and information, that Edward ought to be elected a member of some leading scientific society. There is no such body of greater distinction in the world of science than the Linnean Society; and of this learned institution Edward was duly elected an associate in 1866. The honour was one which he had richly deserved, and which no doubt he fully appreciated.

And yet he was nothing more even now than a working shoemaker, who was earning not more but less wages even than he once used to do. He had brought up a large family honestly and respectably; he had paid his way without running into debt; his children were all growing up; and he had acquired a wide reputation among naturalists as a thoroughly trustworthy observer and an original worker in many different fields of botany and zoology. But his wages were now only eight shillings a week, and his science had brought him, as many people would say, only the barren honour of being an associate of the Linnean Society, or the respected friend of many among the noblest and greatest men of his country. He began life as a shoemaker, and he remained a shoemaker to the end. "Had I pursued money," he said, "with half the ardour and perseverance that I have pursued nature, I have no hesitation in saying that by this time I should have been a rich man."

In 1876, Dr. Smiles, the historian of so many truly great working men, attracted by Edward's remarkable and self-sacrificing life, determined to write the good shoemaker's biography while he was still alive. Edward himself gave Dr. Smiles full particulars as to his early days and his later struggles; and that information the genial biographer wove into a delightful book, from which all the facts here related have been borrowed. The "Life of a Scotch Naturalist" attracted an immense deal of attention when it was first published, and led many people, scientific or otherwise, to feel a deep interest in the man who had thus made himself poor for the love of nature. The result was such a spontaneous expression of generous feeling towards Edward that he was enabled to pass the evening of his days not only in honour, but also in substantial ease and comfort.

And shall we call such a life as this a failure? Shall we speak of it carelessly as unsuccessful? Surely not. Edward had lived his life happily, usefully, and nobly; he had attained the end he set before himself; he had conquered all his difficulties by his indomitable resolution; and he lived to see his just reward in the respect and admiration of all those whose good opinion was worth the having. If he had toiled and moiled all the best days of his life, at some work, perhaps, which did not even benefit in any way his fellow-men; if he had given up all his time to enriching himself anyhow, by fair means or foul; if he had gathered up a great business by crushing out competition and absorbing to himself the honest livelihood of a dozen other men; if he had speculated in stocks and shares, and piled up at last a vast fortune by doubtful transactions, all the world would have said, in its unthinking fashion, that Mr. Edward was a wonderfully successful man. But success in life does not consist in that only, if in that at all. Edward lived for an aim, and that aim he amply attained. He never neglected his home duties or his regular work; but in his stray moments he found time to amass an amount of knowledge which rendered him the intellectual equal of men whose opportunities and education had been far more fortunate than his own. The pleasure he found in his work was the real reward that science gave him. All his life long he had that pleasure: he saw the fields grow green in spring, the birds build nests in early summer, the insects flit before his eyes on autumn evenings, the stoat and hare put on their snow-white coat to his delight in winter weather. And shall we say that the riches he thus beheld spread ever before him were any less real or less satisfying to a soul like his than the mere worldly wealth that other men labour and strive for? Oh no. Thomas Edward was one of those who work for higher and better ends than outward show, and verily he had his reward. The monument raised up to that simple and earnest working shoemaker in the "Life of a Scotch Naturalist" is one of which any scientific worker in the whole world might well be proud. In his old age, he had the meed of public encouragement and public recognition, the one thing that the world at large can add to a scientific worker's happiness; and his name will be long remembered hereafter, when those of more pretentious but less useful labourers are altogether forgotten. How many men whom the world calls successful might gladly have

CPSIA information can be obtained at www.ICGtesting.com
224840LV00007B/282/A